BLOWBACK

BLOWBACK

THE SILENCER SERIES BOOK 4

MIKE RYAN

WWW.MIKERYANBOOKS.COM

1

Langley, Virginia—A meeting had been called to discuss the killing of one of their agents, Agent 17. The Director of National Intelligence, as well as CIA Director Roberts had grown very concerned at the agency's lack of progress in finding 17's killer in the past three months. Though it had been swept under the rug in the public's eye, with 17's cover alias intact, the agency's hierarchy was starting to demand some answers. Attending the meeting were Director Roberts, his top aide, Deputy Director Tomlinson, as well as Executive Director Manning, who was in charge of the day-to-day activities of the agency. They were already in conference when Deputy Director Caldwell, who was in charge of operations and collecting foreign intelligence, came walking in. With him, was Sam Davenport, who was in charge of the Centurion Project. Roberts wasted little time in starting the questions as soon as the two visitors were seated.

"You two know why this meeting was called, right?" Roberts asked.

"Yes, sir. The death of Agent 17," Davenport said.

"I'm getting almost daily queries from the DNI as to why we still have not apprehended somebody in his death. He's killed in broad daylight, in a public airport, and three months later here we are sitting on our hands with no answers. What exactly is being done about this and why has it gotten to this point?"

Caldwell and Davenport looked at each other, unsure who should answer. Finally, Caldwell said. "As far as we can tell, there's been no international chatter indicating someone was coming for him or any type of backlash for any work he's done overseas."

"Nothing at all?"

"We've checked all our sources in every country he's been in, every assignment, but there's nothing to suggest it's an outside source."

"Outside source. Why do you phrase it like that?" Roberts said.

Caldwell looked at Davenport, expecting him to take over from there. Davenport cleared his throat and began talking. "We've come to believe it's some type of personal matter."

"Personal matter. Such as?"

"We're still digging into it."

"You're gonna have to give me something better, Sam," Roberts said. "You obviously have some type of information leading you in that direction."

"It's more theory on our part right now than actual facts."

"OK. Explain how you got there."

"As Director Caldwell said, we've checked every single assignment 17's been on, and there are no red flags, no anomalies, except for one. And it was internal."

"Internal?" Executive Director Manning asked. "You mean somebody who works for us."

"Well, worked. But yeah, that's what we think," Davenport said.

Manning looked less than convinced. "OK. So why?"

"Three years ago, 17 was part of a group of agents that participated in the elimination of one of our Centurion agents in London."

"What were the circumstances?" Roberts said, locking his fingers together as he prepared to listen.

Davenport opened one of the file folders he'd brought with him and took out papers relating to the case, passing them across the table to each man in the room. There were three sheets of paper stapled together, with information about the assignment, Recker's picture, and his bio.

"John Smith was the alias he used while with us. He was a Centurion operative who'd grown tired of his role with the agency and spilled classified information to his girlfriend at the time," Davenport said.

"It says here he was ambushed in London, but somehow survived the attack," Manning said.

"That's right. He was shot, but he killed three of our agents in the process, and wound up in a hospital. Once we got word he was there, and we arrived, he was gone."

"And you never found him again?"

"He disappeared. We didn't get another hit on him

until six months later when he booked a plane ticket to Orlando, Florida."

"For what purpose?" Roberts looked confused.

"That was where his girlfriend lived and was killed," Davenport said.

"And why was she taken out? The information in this report seems sketchy and doesn't really say much."

"Smith had gone to her and told her about his role in Centurion. We thought it was a security risk."

Roberts investigative tail was up as he started grilling for answers. "Why? How do you know? And how do you know he dispensed information to her? Did you have him bugged, tailed, receive a tip, what?"

"No, Smith told us."

"He told you? He just flat out came into your office and told you?"

"Well, he said he was weary of his job and wanted to leave," Davenport said, trawling his memory. "In the course of our discussion, he indicated he had told his girlfriend certain aspects of his employment. Centurion is a top secret black ops project and cannot be revealed to anyone in any sort of fashion. So, we concluded he was becoming unstable and his girlfriend was a non-essential risk we couldn't tolerate."

Roberts held Davenport's eye for a moment. "So, you wouldn't have actually had any such information had he not walked into your office and revealed it, correct?"

"Correct."

"Now does it seem logical a man would do that if he was some sort of risk?"

"We didn't feel it was a risk worth taking."

"And how does 17 play into this?"

"17 was the agent who killed Smith's girlfriend," Davenport said as he wiped his face, a sheen of sweat forming on his forehead.

"And you think now, after all this time, Smith came back and killed him for revenge?" Manning said.

"While we have no proof at the moment, it's a working theory we're pursuing right now, yes."

"So, he just dropped out of sight for six months after London," Roberts said. "Then he popped up on the radar with a plane ticket to Florida. What happened there?"

"He never got off the plane."

"So, he probably creates a ruse to get all the attention down there while he moves in a different direction."

"We believe so."

"And Smith knows 17 killed his girlfriend because…" Manning said.

"Smith called his girlfriend to warn her but 17 answered the phone and they had a brief discussion," Davenport said, squirming in his seat.

"This sounds like it came right out of a movie or something," Roberts said. "Do you have Smith's file on you?"

"Not on me, no."

"Jeff, pull up his file."

"No problem," Manning said, typing into his laptop.

The men continued discussing the specifics of the two cases and threw some more theories into the air for a few more minutes until Manning pulled up Smith's file.

"Coming on the big screen now," Manning said.

They turned their heads to look at the monitor on the wall, a big seventy inch screen displaying Smith's personal information, as well as his Centurion assignments. They made several comments in passing as they perused the information before coming to a final conclusion after they finished.

"Looks as close to a perfect record as you can get," Roberts said. "What made you think he was a risk?"

"Just a feeling and from what he had said to me already," Davenport said.

Roberts sighed as he looked down at the desk and wiped his face with his hand, obviously distraught at what was going on.

"This is a complete mess," the director said. "So, we don't know for sure this is the work of Smith. We're just assuming it is."

"Correct," Davenport said.

"And there's no video surveillance from the airport, surrounding areas, roadways, highways, nothing to implicate him either."

"No, but that would give further credence to the theory that it's him. He'd know how to avoid all those things."

"Can I ask why I'm just hearing about this London thing three years later?" Roberts said. "Why wasn't I informed of this when it happened? Jeff, were you aware of this?"

"I was not," Manning said.

"So, who was informed of this plan, Sam?"

"I informed Director Caldwell of our intentions

before it was carried out and got his approval," Davenport said. He could feel the damp patch of sweat on his back growing with every minute.

"Dean?"

"I was informed of the general circumstances, but did not review the situation in depth. I relied on the information I was given and gave the green light," Caldwell said.

"And what information was that?" Roberts asked.

"That one of our agents had revealed sensitive information to a civilian and approval was asked for to eliminate that agent along with the civilian he had contact with."

Everyone was silent for a minute as Roberts put his elbow on the table and rubbed his forehead as he looked down at the information Davenport had passed around. There was no doubt the director was obviously displeased at how the situation had been handled. After reading a few paragraphs of text, Roberts finally spoke up again.

"I'm a little bit perplexed, and perturbed, at how this entire situation has not crossed my desk before now," he said. "An agent with a near perfect record was terminated, or attempted as such, along with a United States civilian killed, within our country's borders no less, and I'm just hearing about this three years later. Jeff, how is this possible?"

"I can't say, sir. I wasn't informed of it either," Manning said.

"Sam, can you explain why this didn't go up the chain of command?"

"I asked for permission from Director Caldwell and

got it. I figured it was a Centurion issue, and it was handled. Nothing else needed to be said about it," Davenport said.

"For the record, the killing of a civilian within our borders is not a pressing issue that needed to be handled immediately. At least not one who doesn't appear to be much of a threat or flight risk, as this woman was," Roberts said. "I'll give you an agent who's as skilled and lethal as Smith is, maybe there isn't time to go up the ladder. But the woman, that's gotta go across my desk. One hundred percent of the time. Understood?"

"Perfectly, sir."

"Good. Because if you had done so to begin with, I would not have authorized such an action based on the information you've acquired, which is flimsy at best."

"Understood."

"Regardless, it doesn't change the circumstances of whether Smith is responsible for 17's death," Manning said.

"Do we have any idea where Smith may be now?" Roberts said.

"Well, we believe that due to the Orlando plane ticket, he's somewhere in the United States," Davenport said. "Probably on the east coast."

Roberts put his hands together and put them over his eyes and nose as he shook his head, looking like he had a migraine coming on.

"OK, well, regardless of my feelings of what's already gone down, we need to start making some hay on this," Roberts said. "Sam, you're in charge of Centurion, it's your project, it's your men, you find where Smith is. I want you to put resources into it immediately. You'll report directly to Jeff on this and keep him updated every day on your progress, or lack thereof."

"Yes, sir."

"Once you find his location, you're to sit tight on it and bring it to my desk, is that clear?"

"Perfectly."

"If Smith's our man, and he's the one who killed 17, it's not likely he's gonna go down without a fight. We cannot afford to make a bigger mess on top of the one you've already created." Roberts said, pointedly looking around at the other men in the room.

"Can I ask another question?" Manning said. "What's the status of everyone else who was involved in the London operation?"

"In what way?" Davenport asked.

"Well are they alive, dead, what?"

"Well, the three agents who attempted to kill Smith are dead."

"Killed at the scene while trying to terminate him?"

"Correct?"

"Who else?"

"Smith's handler was in London at the time, and there was another agent who was at the girlfriend's house in Florida."

"And they're still alive?" Manning said.

"Yes."

"Hmm."

"What are you thinking, Jeff?" Roberts asked.

"Seems kind of strange. If Smith was out for revenge, don't you think he'd take everyone out, not just one?"

"Maybe the one's all he knew."

"An agent's handler is a personal connection. If he was that pissed, wouldn't you think he'd be at the top of the list?" Manning asked. "I mean, Smith would probably know how or where he could take him out if he wanted."

"The other issue is how Smith would have found out where 17 is located," Roberts said. "He didn't hit him overseas, he hit him where he lives. Somebody got him the information."

"We've checked our infrastructure and we've had no data breaches in regard to his file," Davenport said. "And he's got nobody else in the agency to turn to. We've checked to make sure nobody's made contact with him, and from what we can tell, nobody has. We've even kept tabs on his mentor who's now retired, and they've never met or made contact since all this went down."

"Well right now we're looking like world class buffoons, including me since I wasn't aware of any of this, so you better get the situation under control."

"We will. I would suggest one small thing if I could."

"Which is?"

"If we get a hit on him somewhere, I believe we should take him out immediately," Davenport said. "He's too dangerous to not act right away."

"Sam, you've already bungled one operation, don't make it two." Roberts' warning was clear. "You make a move without clearing it with Jeff or myself and you will pay for it, am I making myself clear?"

"You are."

"It's also very rare for a man, even one as skilled and talented as Smith is, to just vanish without a trace. There's always a bread crumb somewhere. We need to find it. You don't disappear without help. Someone out there knows something. Find them."

2

R ecker strolled into the office a little past nine in the morning, ready to begin work on a new case. He finished his previous assignment the day before by disposing of a man who had planned on murdering his wife for insurance money. Though Recker would have preferred doing away with the man permanently, Jones persuaded him to just temporarily disable the perpetrator until police arrived. Recker left enough evidence behind that Jones had discovered which should have been enough to convict the man, without the need for further violence. As soon as Recker walked in, he noticed Jones seemed to be working rather hard, swiveling from one computer to another almost seamlessly.

"Anything on the horizon?" Recker said.

"A few promising prospects," Jones said. "Probably will take another day or two to flesh them out more until we can take action on them."

"Vacation day today then?"

"Hardly."

"Looks like you're typing away hot and heavy for something that's not imminent."

"There's something which requires immediate attention, just not regarding us," Jones said. "Well, it involves us, more specifically you, but not an upcoming case."

"Did you just speak English?"

"What I'm trying to tell you is something popped up on my Recker Radar."

"Recker Radar? Is that actually a thing?"

"It's what I named my government surveillance software program involving you."

"Oh. Interesting," Recker said. "So, you're telling me my name resurfaced somewhere?"

"It did. Approximately three weeks ago there appears to have been a high-level meeting among several high-ranking CIA officers and directors."

"So? It's common you know. It happens all the time."

"Yes, but just before the meeting, I got a hit on a memo with your John Smith alias. It came from someone named Sam Davenport and was sent to Executive Director Manning and the date was two days before that meeting."

"Was Davenport there?" Recker asked, finally concerned.

"He was as far as I can tell. That's one of the issues I was having as I cannot place exactly what this Davenport's role in the agency is."

"He's in charge of the Centurion Project."

"Then you know him?"

"I do. He's the one I initially talked to about leaving the agency. Who else was at this meeting?"

"I've confirmed Director Roberts and Deputy Director Caldwell so far. There may be more," Jones said.

"Let me see the initial memo and anything else you have."

Recker pulled up a chair next to Jones and anxiously waited for him to pull up the information. It was the first time Jones had seen a concerned look on Recker's face after informing him of a possible breach. Recker had always said he wouldn't really be worried about anyone looking for him unless it was the CIA coming. He knew they were the only ones who really had the capabilities of finding him. And if they really were looking for him, Recker knew it was only a matter of time before they found him. Jones finally pulled up the first memo and let Recker read it for himself.

To: Executive Director Manning
   From: Sam Davenport

Per your request, we still have no leads into 17's death. We believe it likely to be someone with a personal connection to his past. We have several theories, though nothing concrete. We are looking into the possibility of whether it is related to a job he did that involved a former agent of ours, John Smith. I'll keep you updated.

. . .

Sam

Recker quietly sat there reading the memo, analyzing it, studying it to see if there were any hidden meanings behind any of the words as they sometimes liked to do.

"Anything else?" Recker asked after reading the memo several times.

"Yeah."

Jones brought up another memo, somewhat overlapping the first one on the screen. Recker's eyes were glued to the monitor as he began reading.

To: Sam Davenport
From: Executive Director Manning

We need further clarification on what's being done at the moment. Director Roberts is calling every day looking for answers and he's getting impatient at the lack of progress. He's called a meeting for this Wednesday at 10am with you, Director Caldwell, and myself. Bring your files and what you have on this Smith and be prepared to explain your plans going forward.

Executive Director Manning

. . .

After reading it five times, Recker leaned back in his chair, while still staring at the screen. He put his fingers over his mouth and rubbed his lips as he analyzed the memo. By his mannerisms, Jones detected something was bothering Recker.

"What is it?" Jones said. "It looks as though something's got your attention."

"I'm not sure. It's the way the second memo is worded."

"I didn't notice anything strange or out of the ordinary."

"It's the way Manning identifies me," Recker said. "He called me this Smith."

"And the significance is?"

"Well, in the grand scheme of things, I guess it doesn't make a bit of difference. But on a personal level, I always wondered just how far up the order to kill me went."

"And this helps in that?" Jones asked.

"Well, from the sound of it, it doesn't seem like Manning even knew my name."

"How can you be certain?"

"Well, he called me this Smith. It sounds like he didn't know me. Think about it, anytime a person ever says this in front of someone's name, it indicates a lack of familiarity of the subject. If he knew me, he'd just say Smith, not this Smith."

"Very astute observation, Michael."

"Which probably means the order came either from Davenport or Director Caldwell and didn't go any further up."

"Does that help us somehow?"

"If they're looking for us, doesn't help us a bit," Recker said. "But for my own peace of mind, it helps answer a question I always wondered about."

"How reassuring," Jones said.

"When was all this?"

"Looks like the meeting took place a few weeks ago. The memos aren't dated but that would place them approximately two or three days before I assume. Why would they bother with memos at all? Aren't they all located in the same building?"

"No," Recker said. "Centurion headquarters are in New York. Most black ops programs are located somewhere other than Virginia to try to operate in secrecy. Everyone knows where the CIA building in Virginia is, but it's easier to come and go without prying eyes in a completely different area. Especially a high-volume city such as New York where it's easier to blend in. Rent an office building, register a fictitious name and you're up in business."

"So, what do you propose we do about this?"

"Nothing to do yet until they show up. Just keep going about our day like normal and monitor it best we can."

"You seem pretty sure they will be here."

"Part of me has always known I couldn't run from them forever. It's the way this stuff goes. You knew it too. I guess my stunt down there in Ohio just put me back in the forefront," Recker said.

"There's always packing up and leaving."

Recker grimaced, not really keen on the idea. "We've put down roots here, made connections, friends... I don't know if it's in the cards now."

"Roots can be replanted, new connections made, and the only friend we've made here is Mia," Jones said.

"Tyrell too. Besides, I don't plan on running forever."

"So, what, you're just going to bunker down and fight like you're the last man at the Alamo?"

"Either way, this doesn't affect you. They won't find a connection between us. Whenever they find out I'm here, it'd be best if we don't get too close for a while."

"Anything that affects you, affects me," Jones said. "I can't do this on my own, and if you're gone, it would mean I have to find, train, and trust a brand-new person."

"You did it once. You can do it again."

Jones grumbled, not liking the situation one bit. "How much time do you think we have?"

"Depends. The quick version... probably a week or so. If it takes a while... few weeks, couple months at the latest."

"I suppose we both knew this would happen, eventually. I just hoped it wouldn't be for a few more years."

"Probably would have been if I hadn't taken 17 out. It would have put me back on the radar. They're looking for connections and I'm probably the only one who fits."

"Well I suppose the good news is we've got advance warning."

"I'll probably have to get word to Mia to let her know I'll be scarce for a while," Recker said.

Jones started squirming in his seat upon hearing her name, not wanting to reveal he was supposed to be meeting her for lunch. Even though Recker and Mia had a few tender moments after their little escapade in New Jersey a few months before, neither one pursued anything more serious upon their return back home. It'd actually been about two weeks since Recker had heard from Mia, which was highly unusual, considering she used to call or text him at least every other day. Jones played off his concerns by telling his partner he'd been hacking into hospital records periodically and checking Mia's time sheets. He kept telling Recker she was having a heavy workload, even working days off and overtime, which was why he hadn't heard from her much. It was an answer that satisfied Recker for the time being.

Jones was not about to be the one to inform Recker that the reason he hadn't heard from Mia was because she started dating someone else. Even though she had every right to find someone, and she and Recker weren't together, Jones still knew how Recker felt about her. He wasn't sure exactly how Recker would take the news. Maybe he'd be fine. Maybe he'd be angry. Maybe he'd get depressed. Maybe he'd be all those things wrapped up in one package. But Jones wasn't going to be the one to tell him about it. Since Recker and Mia were never together, there was no reason he should've objected to a new relationship of hers, but his feelings for her were a fickle business. Sometimes they changed with the weather and sometimes for what seemed like no reason at all. Maybe it was because Jones knew Recker really felt more for Mia than just being friends and didn't want to be the one who disappointed him, even though Recker himself said things couldn't go further with her. But what he said and what he would actually feel when she actually did move on were two different things.

The only reason Jones even agreed to meet Mia for

lunch at all was because she was really persistent. She was good at it. She never did take no for an answer very well. She contacted Jones almost a week ago to ask if he could meet her for lunch. She wanted to talk to him about her new boyfriend and how to tell Recker about it, if at all. One thing Jones never imagined being when he started up this operation, was the middleman in a love triangle. He reluctantly agreed to meet Mia, mostly because he needed for Recker not to go off the deep end when he found out, and he hoped by talking with her, they could figure out the best way to break it to him.

Once noon came around, Jones started wrapping up his work on the computer. Recker was on one of the other computer stations, trying to figure out his CIA issue. His attention was diverted when he saw Jones stand, appearing like he was going out somewhere. It was pretty unusual behavior for him. Though Jones every now and then would go out for lunch, he never did when there was what appeared to be an urgent situation. And Recker figured this CIA issue could be classified as an urgent situation. Jones usually would work right through lunch and keep himself glued to his chair. So, his leaving right about now struck a chord with Recker.

"Where are you going?" Recker said.

"I have a prior engagement I have to attend."

"An engagement? What, like a party or something?"

"No," Jones said, trying to think of something else to tell him.

"Uh... then where are you going?"

"I'm meeting a contact."

"A contact? Like who?"

"Well, I can't tell you."

"Why?"

"I don't know his name," Jones said, caught in a lie.

"This is highly unusual for you, don't you think? It's usually me meeting contacts."

"Desperate times call for desperate measures."

"I didn't realize we were in desperate times," Recker said.

"Well, alarming times, how's that?"

"You want me to come along for backup?"

"No. Won't be necessary."

"You want me to monitor things from here?"

"No, I'll be fine," Jones said.

"You're being awfully cloak and dagger about this thing."

"As you know, some things have to be kept close to the vest."

"Where'd you find this contact?"

"I can't say. I'll fill you in when I get back."

"Do I have to worry? Dangerous perhaps?"

"No danger involved. It's just an exchange of information," Jones said, hoping it would be enough to quiet Recker down.

Though he wasn't really satisfied with that answer, or any of the other ones that Jones had said, Recker stopped with the questions. He realized that Jones wasn't going to tell him anything useful, so he figured it was best to just let him go. Besides, with the CIA starting to breathe down his neck, Recker didn't have time to worry about more trivial things. If Jones really needed his help, he would've asked.

When Jones got to the restaurant, Mia was already sitting and waiting. Upon seeing her, the Professor looked at his watch and hurried over to her table. Mia gave him a big smile, then stood to give him a warm hug. She had already ordered drinks for the two of them so they took their seats to look at the menu.

"Thanks for coming," Mia said.

"Sorry I'm late." Jones checked his watch. "I got caught up with things, then I hit traffic, then..."

"David, it's OK. I'm just glad you're here."

Jones lifted his drink and looked at the top of it.

"Sweetened iced tea, just the way you like it."

"You know me so well."

"Yeah, it's nice the two of us getting together like this. We should do it more often."

"Yes, I don't remember the last time we did this," Jones said.

"David, we've never done this."

"Oh, nonsense. We've had lunch together plenty of times."

"Yeah, at my apartment, or with you, me, and Mike. But never just us, out somewhere. It's kind of nice. Different."

"It is. So, should we get to the basis of this meeting?" Jones asked.

"Meeting? You make this sound so formal. Can't two friends just sit and have lunch together?"

"Indeed, they can. Our relationship, however, has never been predicated upon lunch dates or social gatherings. You indicated that you wanted advice on your situation with Michael, did you not?"

"Well, yeah."

"Well then, why beat around the bush, or dance around the subject, or pretend it's for some other reason? Friends talk about other friends, right?"

"OK," Mia said, unsure how to proceed.

She stuttered for a minute and started to say something, though no words came out of her mouth. She was very uneasy and nervous talking about the subject at all. But she knew it was better to talk it over with someone else first before approaching Recker with it. And since the only mutual friend they had was Jones, he was the only candidate for the job. Jones could see she was struggling to start the conversation, but he wasn't exactly an expert in love or relationships, so he had no idea how to help her or draw out her feelings on the matter.

"So, you're obviously aware of, uh, my... feelings for Mike," she said, stammering and taking a deep breath as if she was having a panic attack.

"Mia, you don't have to go into any kind of deep explanation of personal emotions," Jones said, trying to calm her down before she passed out or something. "I'm well aware you and Mike have an emotional attachment of sorts, but due to his... career, it is not possible to further explore those feelings you have for each other."

"OK, well, a few weeks ago I met someone."

"And?"

"Well, we went on a few dates and he now wants to date exclusively," Mia said calmly, not really believing she was saying the words.

"And your feelings are?"

"I think I might want to."

"Excellent. I think it's a fabulous idea," Jones said, without hesitation.

"You do?"

"Absolutely. You and Mike have never progressed beyond friends and I think it's time you moved on. You deserve it."

"But you don't even know who it is or what he does or anything," Mia said.

"Well who is he?"

"His name's Josh and he's a lawyer."

"Oh," Jones said, cracking a face.

"Well you don't have to say it like that. He's a really nice guy. He's not like a sleazy lawyer or anything."

"What kind is he?"

"He's a personal injury lawyer," she said. "You know, helps people who are hurt at work and the like."

"And people who spill coffee on themselves at restaurants then sue the restaurant I suppose?"

"No! At least I don't think so. Well, I dunno, but he's a really nice guy."

"Makes good money? Treats you right?"

"Yes. Well, the treating me right part. So far anyway. I'm not sure about the money. I haven't asked about his bank account, but he has his own house and a nice car so I assume he's doing all right."

"As I said, if you're happy, you have my blessings. Are you having doubts about this arrangement?"

"No. I think I want to."

"Why does it sound like you're having misgivings then?" Jones asked.

"I don't know. I guess part of me has always just been

waiting for Mike to come riding in on the white horse and take me away."

"Mia, Mike doesn't own a white horse. And continually waiting for something that in all likelihood will not happen is not going to help either of you move on, especially you."

"I know." She looked downcast as she fiddled with her thumbs.

"If you really have feelings for this Josh, and you think it could possibly lead somewhere you want, then you should try to make it work."

"Should I tell Mike or no?" Mia said.

"You absolutely should tell Mike."

"You wouldn't want to kind of casually mention it to him somehow, would you?"

Jones had taken a sip of his drink, almost spitting it out at her reference. He wiped his mouth with a napkin before answering. "No. No, I would not. I'm here for advice counseling and that is all. I'm not doing the dirty work for you."

"How do you think he'll take it?"

"Well, it sort of depends on what kind of mood he's in. There's really no way of telling in advance. If he takes it well, maybe he'll wish you well and just go back to work like it's no big deal," Jones said.

"And if he takes it badly?"

"Maybe he'll just wish you well then go back to work and shoot somebody."

3

When Jones got back to the office after his luncheon with Mia, he noticed Recker was in the same spot as when he left. Jones wondered if he even moved at all in the couple hours he'd been gone. Recker was staring hard at the computer, barely even paying any attention to Jones since he walked in.

"Have you even moved from that spot since I left?" Jones said.

Recker gave him a quick glance before returning his eyes back to the screen. "There's a lot going on."

"I don't think I've ever seen you so concerned about something before."

"I told you I would never worry until the CIA came looking. This is why."

"Just the same. I think I preferred your carefree attitude."

"So how was your meeting?" Recker asked.

"Uh... good."

"So, what are you trying to hide from me?"

"What? Hide from you?" Jones asked, trying to laugh it off. "What are you talking about?"

"Well, in all the time we've known each other, you've never been so secretive before. Now suddenly you're going off, not telling me where you're going, who you're meeting, seems kind of fishy."

"I'm just not at liberty to reveal their name."

"What was it about?"

"Just a… case."

"A case we're not on," Recker said. "Considering I finished the last one yesterday."

"Well, about the CIA problem."

"And you don't think it's worth sharing?"

Recker could tell Jones was just saying whatever popped into his mind. If it was really about a case, Jones would've just come out and said what it was about. He wouldn't have danced around the subject like he was doing. And if it was really about the CIA, it wasn't something Jones would've kept to himself. So, if it wasn't about a case, or the CIA, then it must've been something personal. Either for Recker or for Jones. With a few suspicions as to what it might've been about, Recker lobbed a few more questions at his friend, just to see how he'd handle them. After a short give and take, Recker thought he might've figured it out. At least partially.

"Is this about Mia?" Recker asked.

"What? Mia? Why would it be about Mia?" Jones asked incredulously.

"Because I haven't heard from her in a week, you're

being ultra secretive, sounds like you two are planning something."

"Don't be ridiculous. What on earth would we be planning?"

"That's a good question. Why don't you answer it?"

"I can't."

"Do I have to call Mia and ask her?"

Jones suddenly looked much more pleasant. "Yes. Yes, I think you should do that."

"If I can ever get her on the phone," Recker said.

Though Jones kept buttoned up and steadfastly refused to confirm anything else, he didn't deny whatever he was hiding had something to do with Mia. For Recker it was basically a confirmation it was true. Recker grabbed his phone and made another call to Mia, once again going to voicemail. This time, he left a message.

"I guess now I know how it feels," Recker said.

"What's that?"

"Trying to call someone repeatedly and not getting an answer. I guess now I know how she's felt these past couple years when she called and I didn't answer."

"Oh. Well, turnabout is fair play as they say," Jones said.

Not having to answer any more questions, Jones sat again and got back to work. With nothing new on the CIA front, he pulled up some of the cases he'd been keeping an eye on lately. As he was working, Recker continued his CIA search, trying to glean any new information he could. After about thirty minutes, Jones made a couple of muffled sounds which distracted Recker. Since the Professor didn't say anything to him, Recker played it off and kept going about his own business. A few minutes later, Jones made the same type of noises, drawing Recker's attention again. He put his elbow on the table and rested his head on his hand staring at his partner, waiting for an explanation of his troubles. Jones didn't even seem to realize what he was doing and never took his eyes off his screen. A few more minutes went by with Recker staring and he finally got tired of waiting for an explanation.

"So, do you wanna spill it?"

Recker's voice finally broke Jones' concentration, and he looked over at his partner. "Hmm?"

"Do you wanna share what's so fascinating about whatever it is you're looking at?"

"I wish it was fascinating," Jones said. "It's more like... disturbing."

"Well, are you going to share?"

"Oh. It's one of the cases I've been monitoring. To be honest, it's one I hoped would just somehow magically go away without us having to get involved. Sadly, it doesn't seem to be the case."

"What's the trouble?"

"It's um..." Jones hesitated, rubbing his head as he thought of the best way to explain it.

Recker didn't recall a case in which Jones had trouble stating the issue before. It was his first tip-off it might be something big. "Just say it."

"Well, it's actually two people I've been keeping an eye on. I first caught wind of a text message one of them sent to the other about... children," Jones said, struggling to get the words out.

"Children? What do you mean, children? What about them?"

"One of them is a convicted child sex offender."

"What's the message say?" Recker asked.

"Well, apparently one of them has been watching an elementary school and has his eyes on a couple of kids. Some of the language they use is... well, I just can't repeat it. Not when thinking about kids. Here, you look at it."

Jones moved his chair over a little so Recker could come in and take a look at what he was seeing. Recker read the messages the two men had been sending to each other regarding the children they were seeking out. Recker had seen and heard a lot of things, and not much really bothered him. But reading what these two men were planning on doing to some small children really disgusted him.

"Who are these creeps?" Recker asked.

"Reed Laine and Sidney Bowman."

"Both convicted sex offenders?"

"Only Laine is. He is not allowed to be anywhere near a school. Bowman on the other hand, does not appear to have any kind of criminal record," Jones said, still clearly bothered by what he had picked up on.

"How do these two jerks know each other?"

"That I do not know off-hand. It appears the two somehow befriended each other somewhere along the line over the years. Maybe online, maybe in a chat room, maybe on a message board, maybe somewhere on the dark web, who knows? I do know they weren't childhood friends. They grew up in different areas, different schools, never worked together. So, my best guess is they hooked up online somewhere due to their fascination with... the kids. That seems to be the tie binding them together."

"Wonderful. Anything concrete on the time and place of what they're planning?"

"Nothing definitive as of yet."

Recker took a few steps back then walked over to his gun cabinet. He selected his two weapons, his primary and backup, as per his usual. As he closed the cabinet, he looked over at Jones, who appeared to be deep in thought. Jones was kind of staring away from the computer toward the wall, not seeming to be looking at anything in particular.

"What is it?" Recker asked.

"I was just thinking if maybe it'd be a good idea if we kept a low profile for a while."

"You mean take a vacation?"

"No. Just work more in the shadows. Relay our information to the authorities, let them handle things," Jones said. "Kind of stay quiet."

"You want us to sit on our hands while these two jerks are out there molesting kids?"

"No. Not at all. We can forward what we have to the police and let them take over the investigation."

"Why?"

"Well, with the CIA looking into your whereabouts again, I just think it may be wise to stay in the background until things blow over a little."

"David, I'm not someone who just sits on my hands very well."

"I'm aware."

"Besides, what can the police do?"

"Monitor their behavior and such."

"Yeah, monitor their behavior after they've already committed some heinous act some poor kid will never emotionally recover from," Recker said.

"I'm not saying we should do nothing."

"I know. You're just saying to let someone else do the dirty work."

"I'm just worried. If something happens, it may put you even more in the spotlight. A spotlight we don't need at the moment," Jones said. "Any type of publicity The Silencer gets at this moment may be something which draws the CIA closer to our doorstep. To your doorstep."

"You can't live in fear, waiting, wondering, hoping something doesn't happen."

"I'm not saying we should be living in fear, I'm just wanting to exercise some caution."

"Listen, I hear you and I understand your concern. But it doesn't really change anything. Do you really wanna put this in the hands of the police and take chances on the lives of children? What if the police can't act on the information you give them? Which is likely. What if they have too much on their plate and they don't get to these creeps in time? You're leaving a lot to chance."

"I know."

"And if this was some run-of-the-mill nut job and innocent children weren't at play, then maybe I'd agree with you. But I won't stand by and let children be targets. I didn't sign up for this to stand on the sidelines."

Jones nodded, completely understanding Recker's position, and actually agreeing with it. Even though he suggested caution, Jones knew his partner was right on point with his arguments and he really had no winning argument against them. Now that they were in agreement that they shouldn't do anything different than usual, Recker went back to the computer to get more information.

"Where am I gonna find these clowns?" Recker asked.

"Reed Laine lives on Washington Street and Sidney Bowman lives on Ashford."

"Do we know what school they're targeting."

"They didn't say. But, judging from where they live and the approximately to the closest school, I can take a guess," Jones said.

Recker took a final look at their addresses to memorize it before heading out to find them. He usually could commit everything to memory, but asked Jones to send him the information just in case.

"Send their pictures and whatnot to my phone," Recker said.

"Mike, if I can give some advice, please handle this as quietly as possible."

"Should I leave them tied up in the middle of a room with some porno mags taped to their chests?" he asked sarcastically.

"I'm just saying discretion is sometimes the better part of valor."

"I'll do what has to be done. No more, no less. Just like always."

Recker bid his partner goodbye and left the office to find their targets. Once he exited the office, Jones got a bad feeling about his intentions.

"Just like always. That's the part I'm worried about,"

Jones muttered.

As Recker drove, Jones forwarded the requested information to his phone. He sent the pictures of the two men, along with their addresses, work information, as well as DMV information on their cars. Everything Recker might possibly need to find the two as quickly as possible, he now had. Considering the two men only lived a few blocks from each other, Recker wouldn't have far to go to find either of them. Recker's first target was Laine, who was the closest. It took Recker about twenty-five minutes to reach the Laine address. Laine lived in a row home in an end unit. There was a small driveway big enough to house one car in the three-story home, though there was no car sitting there. Laine was supposed to be driving a small gray Toyota. Many owners of these homes also parked on the street by the curb due to the lack of space so Recker cruised up and down the street, and even on the connecting streets, just to make sure it wasn't nearby. But it wasn't in sight. Instead of sitting waiting for a while, Recker drove over to the address of Bowman, which was only about five minutes away. He also lived in a similar house, a row home, though his unit was in the middle. Once Recker found the address, he parked across the street. He saw a light blue Ford belonging to Bowman parked in the driveway. While Laine was single and lived by himself, Bowman was living with his parents, as the house was registered in their names.

While the thought occurred to Recker to just burst through the front door and start blasting away, he didn't want to hurt or injure innocent people, which he assumed Bowman's parents to be. Recker called Jones and asked him to run a quick background check on them just to make sure they were unaware of their son's behavior. Recker would just sit tight until Jones got back to him with the information. He also wasn't sure if the parents were even there at the moment. So, while he preferred not to wait at the moment, he figured it was the best strategy for the time being. After uneventfully sitting there for half an hour, Jones got back to him with the information he had requested.

"As far as I can tell, Bowman's parents are not connected to their son's activity in any way," Jones said.

"They don't know anything about it?"

"Well, they know their son has issues, and it looks like they've tried to get him help with psychiatrists and doctors and the like, but it doesn't appear the apple falls from the tree if you get my meaning."

"So, they don't know he's staking out schools and kids right now," Recker said.

"It wouldn't appear so."

That bit of information confirmed Recker's strategy to wait until he could get Bowman alone. Since the parents didn't seem to be involved, he was going to make sure they weren't hurt in whatever went down. Recker still wasn't sure what he was going to do, but everything going through his mind seemed to have a violent end to it. He knew it wasn't what Jones wanted, but in this case, Recker didn't see another way around it. Maybe Jones was right and they should tread carefully, but with kids involved, Recker just wasn't willing to tap dance around. He'd do what he thought was right and let the chips fall where they may.

Two more hours went by and Recker was starting to get a little antsy. Though he didn't usually get anxious over cases, when kids were involved, and not knowing exactly when the two subjects were planning on putting their plans into motion, he was ready to get moving. Fortunately, he didn't have much longer to wait. He saw the front door open, and a man came out of the house. Recker looked at his phone for confirmation it was Bowman. It was. At first glance, Bowman didn't appear to be a very threatening type of guy. He wasn't big or imposing or tough looking. He was in his mid to late forties, rim glasses, and kind of small at five feet four or five. Seeing him for the first time, you wouldn't expect him to be the type who'd have issues like this. But, as Recker was well aware, most people had secrets hidden away. He watched as Bowman locked the door to the house, walked down the steps then got into his car. As he pulled away and drove down the street, Recker followed him, keeping a safe distance behind him so Bowman wouldn't see he was being followed.

After driving for a few minutes, it became clear where Bowman was going. Once he made a left turn at the traffic light, there was an elementary school dead ahead. Bowman drove up to the edge of school property and parked just alongside the curb. It was recess and most of the kids were outside playing. Recker parked about five car lengths behind his target and just sat there watching him. As he sat there, he called Jones to let him know what was happening.

"Well, looks like we know what's on Bowman's mind," Recker said.

"Which is?"

"He just drove down to the elementary school and parked. He's watching the kids at recess."

"That is alarming, isn't it?"

"There's no use in waiting, is there?"

"We could call the police and have them run him off," Jones said.

"What for? You said he has no record. There's nothing stopping him from being near school grounds."

"I'm just searching for an alternative."

"There are no alternatives," Recker said. "You and I both know what has to be done."

Even though Recker seemed strongly in favor of capital punishment, he wasn't as sure in his own mind. It was part of why he called Jones to begin with. Part of him hoped that Jones had another solution at hand, even though Recker knew there was none. He knew what he had to do. Recker partially opened his car door, ready to unleash his brand of justice, but then thought better of it. He heard the joyful screaming of the kids playing in the background and it caused Recker to pause. He then shut his door again as he contemplated a better option. Killing Bowman near school property just didn't seem like the right move. There'd be a big commotion, along with a police presence, news cameras and reporters, and a lot of outside noise that Recker didn't think was fair to subject a bunch of young kids to seeing. Recker would have to wait and pick a better spot. As he continued thinking about his plans, his phone rang. It was Jones.

"Yeah?"

"You haven't done anything yet, have you?" Jones asked.

"No. Not yet. Why?"

"Well, as we've noted, Bowman doesn't have any type of record. It appears his family has tried to get him help for his problem."

"So? We already know all that. What's your point?" Recker said.

"My point is, you don't have to do what we both know you're planning on doing."

"I asked you for alternatives earlier. You didn't have any."

"Well, maybe if you just talked to him, let him know you're watching him, that may be enough to scare him off," Jones said.

"You really think so? People like this are sick. You really believe a good talking to is all he needs? What do you think happened when he visited the psychiatrist?" Recker asked.

"Would it hurt?"

"Well it might not hurt, but it sounds like a complete waste of time. Don't forget we got one more guy out there doing who knows what."

"Believe me, I'm well aware of that."

"You really think a little chat is going to do any good?"

"It's worth a try," Jones said.

Recker let out a little grunt, "Fine. But I'm telling you this is a waste of time."

"Noted."

Recker hung up and quickly got out of his car, not wanting to waste any more time. With his guns tucked firmly out of sight inside the belt of his pants, he closed his car door and took a look around to make sure he wasn't being watched or there was nobody nearby who could see any commotion going on. With the coast clear, Recker started walking toward Bowman's car. As he approached it, he could see Bowman was looking at the school playground through a pair of cheap looking binoculars. Seeing that made Recker even angrier and more agitated than he already was. Still unsure what he was going to do or say, Recker was just kind of making things up as he went along. He stopped when he got alongside the driver side window. Bowman didn't even realize he was there at first. Recker knocked on the window to get his attention. Startled, Bowman jumped in his seat a little when he saw the intimidating looking man standing outside his window.

"What do you want?" Bowman asked without rolling the window down.

Recker tilted his head and pointed at his ears, pretending he couldn't quite make out what Bowman was saying. Agitated, Bowman rolled his window down.

"I said, what do you want?"

"Oh, I was just wondering why you were sitting here looking at little kids," Recker said.

"Go away."

Bowman attempted to roll his window back up but Recker prevented him from doing so at first by putting his hands on the edge of the glass. Eventually though, the force of the power window made him lose his grip, and the window rolled all the way up. Rattled, Bowman reached for the ignition and turned the key in an attempt to leave the scene. Obviously, Recker's attempts for a conversation were not off to a good beginning. Though he could've just let Bowman leave since he was obviously rattled and perhaps Recker thwarted his plans, it just wasn't good enough for Recker. He reached around to his back and withdrew one of his guns and turned it around, holding it by the barrel. Recker then took the weapon and slung it to the side of his head as he viciously brought it back down like a backhanded slap, rapping it against the glass as the window shattered. Bowman stopped what he was doing and put his arms up over his head to protect himself from shards of glass cutting into his face. After a few seconds, Bowman put his arms back down, revealing his face once again to the stranger on the outside. Recker once again swung his weapon in a back-handed manner, this time forcefully hitting Bowman across the bridge of his nose, causing his head to violently snap back against the headrest. Recker then moved the gun to his left hand and reached through the window and unleashed a right cross that caused Bowman to slump across the gear lever in the middle console. Recker pulled the lock up on the inside of the door and opened it, pushing Bowman completely into the passenger seat, though half of his body was on the floor of the seat well. With Bowman in a lot of pain and holding his face due to the blood dripping down from his broken nose, Recker took control of the wheel and peeled out of the parking space.

"Who are you? What do you want?" Bowman yelled, though it was somewhat garbled as his hands were covering his mouth from still holding his nose.

"I'm just a concerned citizen," Recker said.

Recker wasn't exactly sure where he was going, figuring something would occur to him as he was driving. Or maybe, he'd see something which would just stick out to him as a good place to go. His phone started ringing again, though he didn't even check to see who it was, assuming it was Jones, and he didn't especially feel like talking to him again at the moment.

"Where are we going?" Bowman asked.

"Just shut up."

"You broke my nose."

Recker kept his eyes on the road, not feeling bothered at all. "I'm heartbroken."

"Why are you doing this to me?"

Recker didn't respond and instead focused on driving. He noticed Bowman starting to move around a little more, like he was about to get off the floor entirely and get in the seat.

"Just stay where you are or I'll break a few more things," Recker said.

He didn't feel the least bit threatened by the man, but Recker didn't want to take chances and have his passenger try something stupid. Having him kneeling on the floor kept him at a more acceptable distance. After a short drive, Recker saw a small shopping center and pulled in, parking near the outside of it, as far away from the stores as possible. It was a small center that had a grocery store, drug store, pizza shop, as well as a few other small establishments.

"Looks like this is where it ends, sonny," Recker said.

Bowman looked worried. "What are you gonna do

with me?"

"Well, you and your friend Laine seem to have a little problem with looking at the kids, huh?"

"I don't know what you're talking about."

"Do I look stupid to you?"

"No."

"I've seen the messages you two creeps have sent to each other."

"It was nothing," Bowman said, shrugging his shoulders. "We were just kind of kidding around."

"You don't joke about things like that. Besides, if it was just kidding around, you wouldn't have been at the school where I found you, would you?"

"I was just taking a drive and parked for a few minutes. The kids make me feel good."

"Yeah, I bet they do." Recker felt sick to the stomach at the thought of what kind of 'good' the kids made Bowman feel.

"So, what are you gonna do?" Bowman asked, seeing the gun sitting on the seat between Recker's legs.

"Well, I'm supposed to be having a chat with you to tell you never to do it again but I have a feeling it's gonna be useless. Isn't it?"

"I'll do whatever you want."

"Yeah, I kind of figured you'd say that. Then tomorrow when I'm not around anymore you'll find yourself right back in the same situation."

"No. I swear."

Recker sighed, unsure of the point of having the conversation. He could tell it wasn't going anywhere. And like he said, as soon as he was gone, Bowman would be right back to doing the same thing. He wasn't going to change just because of a conversation with Recker. Recker wasn't sure why he even bothered to listen to Jones and try this method first. It was a complete waste of time. He should've just done what he wanted to do in the beginning. Recker grabbed the Glock from between his legs and pointed it at Bowman. Without thinking or blinking, he fired three rounds into his target's chest, killing the man instantly as his face slumped down onto the seat, his shirt soaked in blood.

He didn't want to stay at the scene very long, so Recker quickly got out of the car and started walking back to his. Luckily it wasn't too far away. It'd give him some time to calm down. Shooting someone was never a good feeling, no matter who it was, though Recker knew taking out someone like that was necessary. As he walked, he reached into his pocket and removed his phone to see who had called him. As he suspected, it was Jones. To pass the time, Recker called him back.

"You need something?" Recker asked.

"I was just calling to see how you were making out."

"Good."

"When you say good, you mean?"

"I mean it's done. Onto the next one."

"You talked with Bowman?" Jones said.

"I did. Didn't do a bit of good."

"Oh. So, what happened?"

"What do you think happened? He's dead," Recker said.

"Oh."

"I did what had to be done."

4

I t'd been a few weeks since the meeting in CIA
Director Roberts' office and his patience had
reached its limits. He was mystified and frustrated
that the agency had seemingly made no progress in that
time. He had meetings lined up all day to figure out how
to proceed next. Sam Davenport and his Centurion team
had run out of time in his mind to find either Smith, or
17's killer, or whether or not Smith was responsible for it.
He was ready to try something new. That something was
someone he trusted who could bring a fresh set of eyes to
the situation. Davenport and his crew obviously had no
new leads and had run out of options. Roberts' first
meeting was 9am with a familiar face. His intercom
buzzed with a message from his secretary. It was a few
minutes early, but Roberts asked her to inform him the
moment his visitor arrived.

"Yes?"

"Michelle Lawson is here," his secretary said.

"Send her in."

Lawson was a bit surprised she was going to be seen so soon. She fully expected to have to wait awhile. Not that she was unhappy about it. She was pleased she wasn't going to have to just sit and wonder why she was there for half an hour. She had no advanced warning, and she wasn't given any explanation of what she was doing there. She was told at the last minute to get to Roberts' office immediately. As soon as she opened the door, she was greeted with a smile and a handshake from the director. With his warm and pleasant disposition, she assumed she wasn't in hot water, or getting fired. It'd been a few years since her last encounter with Director Roberts. Her first, and only, meeting with him was in the same very office she was now in. Roberts asked her to sit at his desk as he walked around and did the same now.

"Good to see you again, Shelly," Roberts said.

"Good to see you too, sir. I think."

Roberts smiled. "Relax. You're not in any trouble or anything. I guess you're wondering why I called you here."

"Yeah, a little bit."

"You've done a great job with Project Specter, but to be honest, the project is probably going to be winding down in the next few years."

"Oh?" Lawson said, worried for her future.

"We've got several similar projects going on now, and in the future. We're going to need people to run those projects. And I'm going to need to appoint people I can trust to run them."

"OK?"

"I'm not promising you anything right now, but I'd

like to put you in the mix for those assignments when the time comes. To do that, you need to spread your wings a little bit."

"In what way?"

"You're going to have to expand your horizons and not be just a handler. You're going to have to have more of an influence, a greater position of power and authority."

"How?" she said.

"I would like you to wrap up your work at Specter and become some sort of a freelancer," Roberts said to her. "I'd like you to work on more pressing issues and situations as they arise, then when they're over, move on to the next one. Kind of like a high leverage specialist."

"And I'd have to give up what I'm doing now?"

"Yeah, it'd be too much on your plate to do both."

"How much time do I have? When would this new position start?"

"You'd have to start immediately, such as tomorrow. How much time, well, today."

"Wow. That's quick. Not that I'm not grateful for thinking of me or for the opportunity, but why me? I'm sure there's other people who are more qualified for this," Lawson said.

"Like I said, I want someone I can trust. After the work you've done on Specter and Matthew Cain, I know I can trust you. I know you won't take shortcuts. But Cain hasn't worked for us in two years, Eric Raines is an experienced agent who doesn't need a handler with your expertise, and you need to start thinking about moving up."

"But if we ever have hopes of getting Cain back into the fold, I don't think he'll do it without me."

"You very well may be right about that. But that's a discussion for another day. If that were to ever happen, we'll deal with it when the time comes," Roberts said.

"What's the assignment you want me on?"

Roberts slid a file folder across the desk. Lawson picked it up and started looking through its contents as the director continued explaining.

"Project Centurion," Roberts said. "It was the next thing after Specter. Three months ago, one of their agents, 17, wound up dead not far from his home in Ohio inside an airport. Since then, we've still got no leads, no options, no nothing. Other than theories, which we're swimming in. John Smith, an agent Centurion leadership tried to take out several years ago, is thought to be behind the killing, mostly because 17 killed his girlfriend. At least that's the theory. No proof though."

Lawson intently continued reading the file, trying to get a thorough understanding of what was going on. It was a lot of information being thrust upon her suddenly. These black ops projects were extremely secretive in nature, and nobody outside of the project, other than senior leadership, had any knowledge of any other actively running projects. It was a lot to digest in such a short amount of time.

"So, basically, at the heart of all this, my duties on this assignment would be to find 17's killer, and this John Smith, assuming that it's not the same thing," Lawson said.

"That's it. Sam Davenport, who's in charge of the

Centurion Project, hasn't come up with a damn thing in a month. The DNI is pressing me for information. Information that I can't give him, because we haven't got any."

"Umm, one other thing... reading this file, I, uh... well, what exactly was the reason Smith was targeted to begin with? It's not really clear in this file."

"Apparently, Smith wanted to leave and expressed that desire, and he may or may not have divulged any details to his girlfriend. Davenport deemed that to be a security risk and sought to eliminate him," Roberts said. "This was done without my knowledge or approval. I actually just found out about Smith a month ago myself."

"May I speak freely, sir?"

"Of course."

"This case they have against Smith to begin with is rather..."

"Weak?"

"Yes."

"I agree. And if it had come across my desk at the time it happened, I would not have sanctioned or authorized any action against him. But, well, it's water under the bridge now. Now we have to clean up the mess," Roberts said.

"And what are your orders regarding Smith if I find him?"

"To do what has to be done. To grow into a leadership position, you're going to have to make the ultimate call. You understand?"

"I do. But what if I find Smith and he's not the one who killed 17?" Lawson said.

"Possibly the same thing."

"What if I could bring him back in? The case against him is weak to begin with from what I can see. He could still be a valuable asset to us if I could reach him."

Roberts chuckled and put his hand over his mouth. "It's what I like about you. Not only do you think about the improbable, you don't immediately dismiss the chances it can be done either. Not one other person has even brought up the possibility of bringing Smith back in as part of the team."

"Well, I do have a tendency to think outside the box sometimes."

"And that's why I thought of you for this. And why you need to get out from your handler shoes and expand your horizons. Do you remember the last time you were here?"

"I do."

"You came in here under difficult circumstances, and while some people would be intimidated, you fought for your beliefs. It's always stuck with me."

"It's easy to fight for something you strongly believe in. Especially when it concerns someone's life."

"But not everyone would do that."

"I also knew him. I knew he was innocent. It wouldn't be so easy or clear with someone I don't know. Someone I only know from reading a file."

"It should never be easy. Once it is, it's time to move on."

Lawson sat back in her chair and sighed deeply as she held the file folder, still reading the contents. Like Roberts suggested, this was a big opportunity for her. Hearing Project Specter was on its last legs was a bit startling, but not completely surprising. It was a project with an overabundance of issues over the years, though under new leadership, seemed to be heading back in the right direction. Unfortunately for everyone involved in Specter, though, there'd been a black cloud hanging over its head ever since their former director was indicted and found to act unethically. Several of their top agents had either retired or been transferred to other projects. Lawson moving on would be a big step up in her career. Another opportunity, at least one as strong as this one, might never come along again. The longer she thought about it, the more appealing it became. How many times in one's career does the CIA Director personally offer something like this? Probably never again. Plus, it was a good challenge. After a few more minutes of thought, her mind was pretty much made up.

"Before I make a decision, where would I work, who do I report to...," Lawson began before being interrupted.

"You'll initially work out of New York, not far from your current office. You'll have complete and total access to all Centurion's files and information. As far as who you report to, it's easy, you report to Executive Director Manning and me. That's it. This is yours, you own it, you have everything in Centurion and the agency's power at your disposal. You need something, you order it, you get it."

"And, uh, Davenport, is he going to be... well, I'm sure he's not... does he even know about this yet?"

"Not yet," Roberts said. "And as to whether he's going to be happy about you coming, no, no he won't. But that's immaterial. He'll have to deal with it."

Lawson nodded, still thinking. She knew what she wanted to do, what she thought was the right decision, but there was still something holding her back from saying the words. She never even dreamed about something like this happening, it was sort of a shock.

"Well?" Roberts asked. "What do you think?"

After a brief hesitation, Lawson agreed to the proposition. "I, uh, I accept," she said with a smile.

"Excellent. You can accompany me to my next meeting then."

"Your next meeting?"

"Sam Davenport."

"Oh. I didn't realize I'd be meeting him so soon."

Roberts grinned. "I hoped, maybe anticipated, you'd be saying yes."

"I guess I should call the office and tell them I'm being reassigned?"

"No need. I've already taken the liberty of reaching out to them. As soon as Director Hayes calls me back, I'll explain the situation to him."

Roberts left the office for a while to attend to other matters. He left Lawson behind to continue reading the file so she could get more thoroughly acquainted with the case. She had about twenty more minutes until the meeting with Davenport. Though part of her was excited about the opportunity being presented to her, she was also a little nervous. She was being given control over a top secret black ops project, and even if it was only temporary, it was still a big chance for her to show what she could do. But she also knew she was being thrust upon Davenport at the last minute, and she was taking operational control over his organization on both the Smith and 17 cases. She assumed he wasn't going to be happy at having her come aboard his operation. Lawson wasn't someone who liked conflict or enjoyed wrestling for power over people and she could only imagine how many cold shoulders or evil looks she was going to receive. Working for a black ops project herself, she knew that if someone was suddenly thrust in to take over Project Specter, they probably wouldn't be too well received either. It'd basically be a vote of no confidence on the current leadership. Otherwise, there'd be no need to bring a new person along.

After reading the file for close to half an hour, Lawson looked up at the clock on the wall and noticed it was past the meeting start time. She wondered what the hold-up was. Maybe they were prepping Davenport for her taking over control, she thought. Whatever the reason, she was getting pretty anxious to get it over with so she could start working on the assignment. A few minutes later, Director Roberts came back into the office.

"Davenport is in the conference room waiting for us. Are you ready?" Roberts asked.

"As ready as I'll ever be."

Lawson quickly shuffled the papers back inside the folder and scooped it up off the desk and scurried out of the office, closely following the director. Along the way to the conference room, she asked a few more questions, wondering about Davenport's personality.

"What kind of person is he?" Lawson asked.

"Well, a little hard-headed, probably overeager, but

also someone who wants to do a good job. Not overbearing, not soft, usually even-tempered."

"Sounds wonderful."

Roberts looked back at her and smiled. "You've worked for worse."

"Good point."

"Besides, this is your operation. You don't need to take bullshit from anyone. If there's any crap that needs to be dished, I want you to be the one throwing it."

"Understood."

Roberts opened the door to the conference room and walked in, Lawson still closely following him. Already seated in the room were Executive Director Manning, Davenport, and Director Caldwell. Only Manning was aware of what was about to go down. Davenport and Caldwell were not in the loop as to the director's plans and were not given any inclination of what this meeting was about. Roberts made a quick, unfriendly type of greeting and walked around to his seat.

"Shelly," Roberts said, directing her to a chair.

Lawson sat next to Manning, as she was told. Across from her was who she assumed to be Davenport. She had seen Caldwell's picture before from other materials distributed within Specter. Since he was in charge of foreign operations, he technically had control of all secret black ops projects and was supposed to be aware of what they all were doing, though he didn't oversee the day-to-day operations of any of them. The day to day duties of Centurion were left up to Davenport. With a legal pad in front of him, Roberts briefly looked at his notes before commencing.

"I'm not gonna beat around the bush here," Roberts said. "The reason for this meeting is there's going to be a little bit of a shakeup, a little change as to the direction of Centurion. Jeff and I have talked at length about this over the past couple of weeks and we both feel, due to the lack of progress in either finding John Smith, or the killer of 17, we need to go in a different direction. From this very moment, Michelle Lawson will take over in those duties. She will have absolute power in those two cases, which may or may not be linked, and will be given complete access to Centurion offices, files, computers, etc. Sam will still have command over all other Centurion business and can focus on those other duties more thoroughly without being distracted with these other things on his plate."

"Sir, it really wasn't much of a distraction," Davenport said.

"Nevertheless, this is the decision we've made, and you'll support Ms. Lawson in whatever she needs, wants, requests, and so forth."

"Absolutely."

Lawson took turns between looking at Roberts and Davenport, who was obviously not pleased at being replaced in these matters. She imagined she'd probably feel the same way if someone was brought in above her to work on something she wasn't having much luck in.

"Dean, I don't know how well you know Shelly, but do you have any objections you'd like to raise on this?" Roberts asked.

Caldwell quickly shook his head. "No. No objections. I'm well aware of Shelly's reputation since Project Specter fell under my umbrella. I've never had the pleasure of meeting her until now, but I'm well aware of her work."

"May I ask what exactly are her qualifications for this?" Davenport said, still a little peeved about being bypassed. "How does this Project Specter compare?"

"Project Specter was the precursor to Centurion," Roberts said. "Some of what we learned from it became the basis of what Centurion was founded upon. What worked well became part of it, what didn't fell by the wayside. She's handled some of the toughest agents you can imagine."

Davenport scrunched his eyebrows together as he tried to understand what the director was telling him. "Are you saying she's just a handler?"

"Not just a handler, Mr. Davenport. She's been the handler of some of the most lethal and dangerous agents this agency has ever seen. Not to mention that she also already has experience in these types of matters. She's already been part of a team that tracked down former members of the CIA who went rogue and into hiding. Her team flushed those men out and brought them to justice."

"It was a group effort," Lawson said, almost sounding embarrassed about being thought of so highly. "Wasn't just me."

Roberts looked at her and smiled before turning his attention back to the Centurion leader. "So you see, Mr. Davenport, she's not just a handler. She has experience in these matters. And quite frankly, her agent handling days I'd say are behind her. Not that this has any importance to you, but she's moving up and could be being groomed for a leadership position in another black ops project which is in the works. She's here because she deserves it and because she's earned it."

"Understood, sir."

"Besides that, her work is exemplary. She has an outstanding attention to detail, works hard, and is very competent in her work. Something lacking at times in other individuals or agencies that won't be named at the moment," Roberts said, hinting at his obvious displeasure.

Davenport gave a single nod of his head, getting the clue that he wasn't the most popular guy in the agency at the moment. They continued talking for close to an hour, going over different strategies, as well as what had already been done so Lawson wouldn't duplicate any of their efforts. It was a tall order, but by the end of the meeting, everybody was impressed by her ideas and were sure that Lawson was up to the task.

5

Recker walked into the office and immediately headed for the coffee machine. Though he hadn't yet looked at Jones, he could almost feel the Professor's icy stare sliding down his back. Recker had already seen the morning newspaper and noticed a story on the inside detailing the murder of Sidney Bowman from the day before. Recker knew Jones was going to give him the third degree any minute. He was waiting for it. But in Recker's mind, at least the story wasn't on the front page. Not that it really deflected the heat off him anymore. As soon as the machine filled his cup, Recker grabbed it and turned around, leaning against the table. He looked over at the computer station and saw the daggers of Jones' eyes piercing a hole through him. It was the meanest, toughest, most aggravating looking face Recker could ever remember Jones having towards his actions.

"If you got something on your mind, might as well just say it," Recker said, sipping his coffee.

"Is it that you believe you're untouchable, or is it that you just don't care?"

"Neither."

"Oh really?" Jones asked. Recker had never seen him look quite so grumpy. "Knowing the CIA has once again put you on the radar, you'd think you'd act in a much more cautious manner than you do. You're reckless, like you have no care in the world."

"I told you, I'm not gonna change the way I behave or how I do business. Killing this guy isn't going to change whether or not the CIA finds me."

"Well it certainly won't hurt their chances. Did you even talk to Bowman at all?"

"Sure I did."

"I mean, did you really talk to him? Did you try to give him an out? Did you try to do things a different way? Or did you ask him one question then make up your mind it was a lost cause and just start blasting away?"

"David, it was a lost cause. People like him are sick. Talking to me isn't going to suddenly scare him straight. If you honestly believe that it would, you're living in a fantasy world," Recker said.

"I just wish you'd exercise some restraint." Jones sighed. "There's already a ton of theories floating around online about the culprit."

"Yeah? Who do they think did it?"

"Well, considering Bowman has no record and no gang affiliations, people are assuming it's not a personal vendetta. Carjacking and kidnapping seems to be the prevailing opinion so far."

"Neither of which would point to me."

"Except he was killed in a way that points to some sort of vigilante justice. There was no attempt to hide the body, or the car, or anything. And who in this city is the leader in vigilante justice?"

"Let me guess... me?"

"I wish I had a prize to offer you for your correct assessment."

"Only prize I need right now is finding the other creep," Recker said.

"Speaking of which, what are your intentions with Mr. Laine?"

"You really need to ask? You already know what my intentions are. He's gonna be joining his friend in the afterlife."

"I had a feeling that would be your response."

"Don't even tell me you're gonna try to talk me out of it. With Bowman, maybe I get it, no record or anything. Laine, though, is a different story altogether. He's got a record for this exact thing. He's not changing his ways, or finding Jesus, or becoming an altar boy, this is who he is. And he needs to be stopped. By any means necessary."

Jones didn't fight Recker's assertion. He knew he couldn't win anyway, even if he tried. But mostly, it was because in this instance, he thought Recker was right. Bowman was different, at least in his mind. He had no record, no history of violence, Jones thought there was a chance he could have been steered in a different direction with a different tactic. Laine, on the other hand, was a convicted child sex abuser, who'd also had numerous other brushes with the law and had been arrested for several other infractions. Laine was now in his mid-forties and had his first brush with the law at the age of sixteen. Jones didn't have any false beliefs about him changing his ways at this stage of the game. He knew Laine was most likely just hours away from meeting the same demise as his friend. And he wasn't going to try to fight Recker on it. The only hope Jones had was that Laine's death wasn't quite as media friendly as Bowman's was. He feared another death as public as the first one would somehow catch the attention of the CIA's radar. The only plea Jones now had was to beg Recker to keep the event as quiet as possible. At least as quiet as any death could be.

"Isn't there a way you can make it look like a robbery or something?" Jones said.

"Huh?" Recker asked, surprised at the question.

"I'd just like to keep the heat off for as long as possible. Another violent death will not help in that regard."

"Does it really matter?"

Jones shrugged. "One never knows."

"At some point the police are gonna connect the dots and figure out that these two jerks knew each other. They're eventually gonna find those text messages, same as you did. They're going to piece together that these two deaths are somehow related."

"Yes, well, anyway, I did some more digging on our friend and it looks like the reason you couldn't find him yesterday was because he has a second job."

"Which is?"

"Bouncer at a nightclub downtown."

"Guess I'm going clubbing tonight," Recker said.

"Maybe you should go home and rest up for a while."

"You trying to get rid of me?"

"Of course not. But that's the only case on our agenda right now and there's not much else for you to do that I can see."

"I can check into my old CIA friends."

"I've got a handle on it," Jones said.

"You are trying to get rid of me."

Jones was about to offer a retort but was interrupted before he could get started by Recker's phone ringing.

"Your saving grace," Recker said, waving his phone in the air. He was pleased to see it was Mia calling, since he hadn't talked to her in a while. "Hey stranger."

"Hi. I know you've been trying to check in with me lately, it's just, uh, I've been busy with work and things."

"Ah, no biggie. Everything good?"

"Yeah, everything's fine. Works busy, but normal."

"Good. Off today?"

"Uh, no. Umm, are you free today by chance?" Mia said.

"Well, looks like I might be. David's kicking me out of the office so it looks like my calendar's been cleared. Why? What's up?"

"Well, I'm about to go to lunch in about half an hour. Can you meet me at the hospital?"

"Yeah, I guess I could."

"OK. See you in a bit then."

Recker hung up and just stared straight ahead for a minute, thinking about the conversation he just had. Something seemed off about it. Mia wasn't talking like her normal self. It seemed like she had something on her mind.

"Leaving, are you?" Jones asked, overhearing the conversation.

Recker shrugged. "Looks that way."

"Well, have fun."

"You happen to know what it's about?"

"What?"

"Mia wants me to meet her at the hospital for lunch."

"And the problem is?"

"Didn't say there was a problem. Just seemed like she was talking like a person with something heavy on her mind," Recker said.

"I guess you'll know when you get there," Jones said, sounding unconcerned, though he had an idea what the subject was about.

Though Recker still was slightly concerned about Mia's tone of voice, at least he didn't have long to wait and think about it. He immediately left the office and drove down to the hospital. When he got to the cafeteria, he looked around and saw Mia already sitting at a table. It was towards the back in the corner. Recker walked around a few tables on his way and noticed a troubling look on Mia's face. She hadn't noticed he was there yet, probably because she was looking down the entire time and didn't even lift her head up once. She jumped a little when she finally noticed Recker, when he was standing right in front of her.

"Oh, I didn't even see you come in," she said.

"I'm not surprised. It didn't look like you'd see a train barreling at you."

"Huh?"

"It's nothing," Recker said. "So, what's the trouble?"

"Trouble? What makes you think there's trouble?"

"Well the look on your face for one. Looks like you're worried about something."

"Well, it's not really trouble. Umm, I just need...," Mia said, scratching the side of her neck as she stuttered and tried to think of the best way to tell him her news.

Recker reached across the table and grabbed her hand in an attempt to settle her nerves. "Mia, you can tell me anything. You know that, right?"

"Yeah. I just don't, um, I don't know how you'll take it."

"Take what? What's this about?"

"Umm, I'm, uh, kind of seeing someone."

Recker took his hand off hers and brought it back in front of him, fiddling around with his fingers as he processed Mia's news.

"Oh. Well that's, um, that's great," Recker said, faking a smile.

Mia could tell he was a little stunned by her revelation, but she knew dragging it out any longer would just make it worse.

"So, who's the lucky guy?" Recker said.

"His name is Josh. He's a lawyer."

"A lawyer?"

"Why does everyone say the same thing? What's wrong with being a lawyer? You know, David had...," she said, quickly shutting up when she realized what it was she was revealing.

"David had what?"

Mia nonchalantly shook her head as she figured how

she was going to get out of the hole she just stepped in. "Nothing."

"David said the same thing? Is that it?"

Mia closed her eyes and nodded, knowing she couldn't lie to him. Even if she tried, she knew he was good at digging out the truth from people. There was no point in trying to hide it.

"You told David before me?" Recker asked.

"I just wanted to get his opinion first."

"Why?"

"Cause I wanted to see what he thought on how well you'd take it. I didn't want you to be mad or anything," Mia said.

Recker looked at a few nearby tables and the people sitting at them as he digested the news she just fed him. Mia was pleasantly surprised at how well he was taking it so far. He didn't seem angry, his face wasn't turning different shades of red, and his voice didn't indicate any level of discontent. He actually seemed somewhat indifferent to the news. As Recker thought about Mia dating someone else, one piece of him was a little sad. He wished he could've been there for her and provided her with a normal life. But he knew he couldn't and he never would. Even though he was slightly disappointed, he didn't want to show it. He didn't have the right to get mad. Not with how he always tried to keep her at a distance. He cared about her too much. It was for her own good to move on from him.

"So, how'd you meet this guy?" Recker asked.

"Uh, he was actually here for something, I think his sister had a baby, and we bumped into each other."

"And he just happened to ask you out?"

"Yeah, pretty much."

"Hmm."

"What's that supposed to mean?" Mia said.

"Nothing. So, when do I get to meet this guy?"

"What?"

"Well, we're friends, right? I'd like to meet him. I just wanna make sure I think he's right for you and all."

Mia seemed a bit taken aback by his request. She hadn't accounted for Recker wanting to meet her new beau and hadn't even thought of it for a second. She figured Recker would never want to meet someone she was dating. Unless it was to punch his lights out.

"What? What's the matter?" Recker asked.

"I, uh, just hadn't expected such a calm response out of you."

"Why? You and David thought I might go out and shoot somebody or something?"

"Umm, well, actually, we did wonder."

"I know. I sometimes have... issues. But I think it'll probably be good for you to date someone."

"You do?" Mia asked, surprised he was taking the news so well.

"Look, I think we both know the way we feel about each other, we've talked about it enough. But you also know why it's best we go in other directions. If I can't give you what you need, then you need to get it somewhere else. I understand. I get it. It's what you deserve."

"Well, I'm glad you approve."

"I do. Just as long as I meet the guy and give him my seal of approval."

"Uh, I don't know. I'm not sure it's a good idea," Mia said.

"Why? What are you afraid of?"

Mia let out a laugh. "Are you serious? What am I afraid of? Do you not know who you are?"

"OK. I know. I'm not gonna shoot him. I'm not gonna throw him off a roof or in front of a moving car. I just wanna meet him and make sure he's good enough for you."

"See, that's what I'm afraid of right there." She grinned. "You wanna make sure he's good enough for me. You're either gonna grill him, or intimidate him, or do something to scare him off."

"Mia," Recker said, putting his hands on his chest, feigning being offended. "You really think I'm gonna do something to scare this guy off?"

"Mmm, yes. Yes, I do."

"I promise you I'll be on my best behavior and I'll do nothing to embarrass you."

"I dunno. I'll think about it."

"So how long have you known this guy?" Recker said.

"You keep calling him this guy. He has a name."

"Oh. Sorry. So how long have you known this guy, Gary?"

"Josh," Mia said.

"Whatever."

"I dunno. Few weeks I guess."

"And you're getting serious about him already?"

"See, I knew you'd do this. You're already grilling me about him. It's why I was afraid to say anything to you."

"OK. OK. I'm sorry. I just wanna make sure... I guess

it's just my protective nature in general, and also of you. I'm always gonna try to protect you. At least, as long as I'm in your life. I just wanna make sure you're getting into a good situation."

"I know. And that's one of the things I've always loved about you. How you look after me. But Josh is a really good guy."

"So, when do I meet him?"

Mia sighed. "I don't know. I'll see."

They continued talking for a few more minutes before they were interrupted, a voice yelling Mia's name in the distance. Recker turned his head around to see who it was, figuring it was a doctor or nurse, or maybe someone from the hospital staff. It was a younger man, though, dressed in a nice suit, in his early to mid-thirties.

"Oh my," Mia said, her mouth dropping open. "What is he doing here?"

She couldn't believe what she was seeing. Before getting up the nerve to ask Recker to lunch and spring on him the news about her new boyfriend, she had originally asked Josh to meet her. He had something come up at the last minute though and canceled on her. So, Mia figured it was as good a time as any to tell Recker about him. She never dreamed Josh would wind up coming anyway, while she was still having lunch with Recker. It was a nightmare of epic proportions. She had to have the worst luck in the world, she thought. Recker turned his head back toward Mia and gave her a little devilish smile. With the garish look on her face and how stunned she looked, he figured he had a pretty good idea who it was calling her name.

"Is, uh, this the new boy toy?" Recker asked sarcastically.

"Oh, please stop," Mia said, worrying already that she was about to have the worst moment of her life.

Recker turned his head back toward the visitor, watching his every move as he walked toward their table. Mia stood to welcome her new boyfriend, though Recker stayed seated as Josh gave her a kiss on the cheek. Josh took the seat next to Mia, who was still shocked they were all together.

"Surprised to see me?" Josh asked.

"You have no idea," Mia said shakily. "What are you doing here? I thought you said you had a last-minute appointment."

"I did. I thought it was gonna take a lot longer though. I wrapped it up fairly quickly. I figured I'd come down and surprise you."

Mia forced a smile, still incredibly uncomfortable with the two men sitting at the same table. "You definitely did."

Josh looked at the man sitting across from them and reached his hand out to introduce himself. "Hi. I'm Josh."

"Mike," Recker said, shaking hands.

"Oh. Mike. Are you the security guy she's friends with that she told me about?"

"I dunno. Am I the security guy, Mia?"

Mia put her elbow on the table and started rubbing the side of her head. "Uh, yeah, yeah. This is my friend Mike. Works in security."

"So, I hear you're a lawyer," Recker said.

"Yeah." Josh laughed. "You don't have to say it like that though. We all gotta make a living somehow, right?"

"Sure do," Recker said, disliking the man almost instantly.

"So, what kind of security work do you do? Mia said it's really dangerous stuff."

"Yeah, it can be. We do security work, investigations, you know. We take on all sorts of clients, usually those in urgent need of protection."

"Hey, if you're ever looking for a job, my firm's always looking for good investigators."

"I think I'm good where I'm at right now."

"You sure? Probably a little safer work than what you're doing now, you know?"

"Most likely. But I doubt I'd get as much satisfaction out of it," Recker said.

"Ah, you're one of those guys, huh? Live for the rush?"

Recker faked a laugh, though he wasn't amused. "No, not really."

"So, how'd you guys meet?" Josh asked. "Mia said you two are close and you've known each other a couple years. But she just won't tell me how you two met."

"I told you that his cases are classified and I can't talk about them," Mia said.

"I think I can divulge this one," Recker said, smiling at her. "Mia had an abusive ex-boyfriend that was stalking her."

"Oh wow. You never told me that," Josh said to her.

"Yeah, I was trying not to."

"So anyway, Mia's father hired me to tail her and watch over her. So that's basically how we met."

"That's great. So, you protected her against this guy and you became friends," Josh said.

"Basically."

"So, what happened to the guy? Did he go to jail?"

Recker smiled at Mia again, almost proud to recall and tell the story. "No, not quite. He had a little bit of a more... extreme end."

"Really? What happened?"

"I threw him off a roof," Recker said bluntly.

Josh laughed, thinking Recker was joking with him. By the look on his face, though, as well as the nauseated look attached to Mia's face, he quickly came to the conclusion it was no joke.

"Wait. You're joking, right?" Josh asked. "I mean, you didn't really throw him off a roof, did you?"

"Well, there's a difference of opinion amongst some of us," Recker said. "Some say he slipped. Some say he was thrown. I like to go with the latter."

"Oh. Well um... so do you usually end your cases like that?"

"Sometimes. Sometimes I just like to shoot them and be done with it."

"Oh my god," Mia whispered, low enough that nobody could actually hear her.

She closed her eyes, thinking this meeting could not have been going any worse. She put her hand over her mouth and shook her head, wondering why she deserved a fate like this.

"So uh, have you had any legal trouble in your work?" Josh said.

"No, why?"

"Oh, nothing, no reason. Just wondering."

"Interested in representing me if the need arises?" Recker asked.

"Oh, no, I'm not that type of lawyer. I do personal injury, workers' compensation, things like that."

"Oh. Mia told me you were a real lawyer."

With Recker's last line, Mia buried her head in her hands even deeper, just wanting to crawl down into a hole and hide for a while. She just wanted to be out of there and go anywhere else.

"Well I am a real lawyer," Josh said.

Recker laughed, slapping the table. "Just kidding with you, man. Of course you are."

"Oh." Josh smiled.

Mia couldn't take anymore. If she stayed there any longer with those two bantering like they were, she might've been driven crazy. Not to mention completely embarrassed. This was exactly the reason why she didn't want the two of them meeting yet. This was what she feared happening. Mia looked at her watch to end the engagement.

"Oh, look at the time. I'm late to get back," she said hurriedly, standing from her chair.

"Already?" Recker asked.

"Yes. I was only on a short lunch."

"Don't you two have to get back to work, anyway?"

"No," Recker said, shaking his head. "Remember, my calendar was clear for the day."

"Oh."

"Well if you have to go, maybe Josh and I can just keep sitting here, talking, getting to know each other."

"Uh, no, no, no, no," Mia said, flustered at another nightmarish scenario. "Uh, you have to get back to work. I know you do," she said, talking to her boyfriend.

"Yeah, unfortunately I have a few more appointments booked for the day," Josh said.

"Ahh, that's a shame," Recker said. He was enjoying himself.

"Isn't it?" Mia asked sarcastically.

"Maybe we can all get together again soon," Josh said, shaking Recker's hand as he stood.

"I'd like nothing better."

6

New York---Lawson entered the Centurion building, a six-story building located in the heart of New York City. There was a receptionist sitting at a desk in the center of the lobby. There were all glass walls dividing the lobby, coming out from the middle of both sides of the desk to the far side of each wall. There was also a glass door on the one side requiring a card to be swiped to go through it.

"Can I help you?" the receptionist asked.

"I'm here to see Mr. Davenport, please."

"And you are?"

"Michelle Lawson. I'm expected."

"Oh, yes. Just go through the door over there and up to the sixth floor, that's Mr. Davenport's office. He's expecting you. Were you given a key card?" The receptionist pointed Lawson to the correct door.

"Yes, I have it," Lawson said, rummaging through her purse to extract the card from it.

"Good. Just swipe it through the card reader attached to the door."

"Great. Thank you."

Lawson swiped her card, which was given to her at the last meeting she had at Director Roberts' office. She was a little surprised at the lack of a security guard in the building so far, but she guessed it helped with whatever their cover was. Nobody would go in there who wasn't supposed to be there, and the glass was bulletproof, so she supposed there was no need for a security presence, anyway. She got in the elevator and went up to the sixth floor, wondering what type of reception she was going to get. She assumed it'd be a little chilly as she knew Davenport wasn't exactly excited about her being there. But she wasn't there to make friends, so it didn't concern her too much. As long as she got what she needed, she wouldn't have to stay there too long. She wandered down the halls for a minute after she got off the elevator, unsure where she should've been going. She passed by a few offices, also encased in glass. She also passed by a door marked "Situation Room", which seemed to be the only door and room which couldn't be seen from the outside. Glass rooms and doors seemed to be the norm in the building, except for the Situation Room, which she could only guess was for high priority meetings or important events. A few people briskly walked past her, most not paying much attention to her. One man slowly walked past her, an open file folder in both hands as he read its contents. He briefly poked his head up and came to a sudden stop as he noticed the strange woman standing there.

"Help you?" the man asked.

"Yeah. I'm looking for Sam Davenport's office."

"Oh," he said, turning around, and pointing down the hall. "Make the first left there, his office is on the right."

"Thank you so much."

"You bet."

Lawson walked down the hall and turned left at the corner and quickly saw Davenport's office on the right. She looked at the door and saw his name written on it, though there was a woman sitting at a desk inside. It was a small room not much bigger than a walk-in closet and there was another closed door towards the middle of the room. Lawson guessed this was his secretary's office or something, or just a way to keep people from getting to Davenport he didn't want to see. Lawson went in and was immediately greeted by the woman.

"Can I help you?"

"Sam Davenport," Lawson said.

"And you are?"

"Michelle Lawson."

"One moment."

The woman held the phone and called into the office to let Davenport know he had a visitor. Once he approved it, the woman hit a buzzer located underneath the desk to unlock the door. Once it started going off, the woman directed Lawson to open the door. She barely got both feet inside the door and hadn't even gotten a chance to close it yet when Davenport hurriedly walked around his desk to greet her.

"I'd offer you something but you won't be here long enough," Davenport said, walking past her. "Follow me."

"Uh, OK," Lawson said, unsure what was going on.

Lawson followed Davenport out of the office and made a right down the hall, then walked down the end of another hallway before making a left, then down another hallway before Davenport turned into another office. He turned on a light as the two entered and removed a few books from a dust-covered desk.

"This is where you'll work out of while you're here, which I hope won't be too long," Davenport said, clearly not pleased to be seeing her.

"Looks like it's seen better days."

"Yeah, it hasn't been used for a while but it's the only office we have available right now."

"It'll do," Lawson said.

"Yeah, it's got a desk and a computer, what else do you need, right?" Davenport asked, making light of it.

"Plus, I brought my own laptop so I'll be fine," Lawson said, putting her computer bag on the desk.

"Great. Anything else you need?"

"Uh, no I don't think so. Well, I could use all the files you have on both Smith and 17, personal, work, whatever."

"Sure. I'll have my secretary bring them over and she'll give you the passwords for our software system as well," Davenport said.

"Thanks. Look, I know you're not real happy about me being here, but it wasn't my idea either."

"It's fine. All that matters is getting the job done, right?"

"Right."

With Lawson squared away, Davenport walked back out of the office, and despite his best efforts to say otherwise, she knew he wasn't happy she was there. But he was giving her what she needed, so it was the only thing that really mattered. Lawson set up her laptop and started going through some of the papers she had, Davenport's secretary coming in only a few minutes later to deliver the rest of what she needed. Lawson devoured everything available to her, studying every single piece of paper they had on both men, reading the same information several times over to get a better understanding of the agents involved. She worked right through lunch and dinner, not even paying much attention to the time, and considering she seemed to be at the very end of the building, there was no foot traffic going by to distract her. She read every report the two agents ever made, every evaluation that was done on them, looked at their physical records, read their comprehensive reports on the Centurion software program and came to one conclusion. If John Smith was 17's killer, finding him was not going to be an easy task. But she still needed more information, something she couldn't find in the reports. She walked out of her makeshift office and went down the hallway, making a few turns until she found herself back in front of Davenport's office. She wasn't even sure he'd still be in there, but once Lawson saw his secretary, figured the boss was still working. After getting clearance, Lawson was once again buzzed in. This time, Davenport was seated at his desk and didn't make a move to get up.

"Something else you need?" Davenport asked.

"I would like to talk to whoever it is you guys use to evaluate these agents."

"Why?"

"Well, it seems to be the only thing missing in those reports."

"What exactly is it you want?"

"I wanna talk to either their handlers or the psych evaluation expert you use," Lawson said.

"For what purpose? I don't understand what it's gonna get you?"

"I wanna get a deeper understanding of who these men are. There's only so much you can learn about someone from a piece of paper. I've never met them before, but the psych guy has."

"17's dead. What else do you need to learn?"

"But Smith isn't. He's out there somewhere and if I can get inside his head a little, maybe I can pinpoint where he is."

Davenport smiled, thinking she was way out of her league. "You know, no matter who you talk to, whatever you read, it isn't going to bring you closer to finding John Smith. He's a world class operator who isn't going to be found by some pencil pusher."

"That's what you think of me as? A pencil pusher?" Lawson asked.

"Look, you strike me as a nice person. Maybe you've worked on some important things and been a good handler to a few agents. But nobody outside this project is just going to waltz in here and find John Smith at the snap of their fingers," Davenport said. "You know when he'll be found? When he wants to be."

"Since we seem to be laying all our cards out on the table, perhaps you can explain to me your reasoning for trying to terminate him to begin with?"

"It's all in the reports."

"No, it's not. You really expect me to believe you tried to kill him just because he wanted to quit and go live with his girlfriend? Do I look like an idiot? Smith had an exemplary record. No verbal warnings, no written counselings, drew tough assignments, had over a ninety percent completion record, and you decided to get rid of him on a whim."

"It's in the report, I've said it before, we viewed him as a security risk," Davenport said tersely. "Yes, he was a good agent. But in our view, he was breaking down, he was starting to go haywire. He was starting to lose focus on his assignments, his mind was elsewhere, he wasn't giving everything he could in our estimation. He'd already told his girlfriend he worked for the government. It was our belief, as time went on, he'd divulge more critical information. Sure, right then, he wasn't a threat to us. But in five years, ten years, the longer he was out, the more classified information he could reveal. I decided it wasn't worth the risk so I put out the order so we would never have to worry about him. Does that satisfy you?"

"Not really. I mean, it's been what, three years now?"

"Yeah. So?"

"Well, has there ever been any indication he's leaked any secret information since he's been gone?"

"It's always easier to second guess when you don't have a foot in the game."

"Maybe so. But considering what you tried to do to him, if he hasn't told any secrets by now, I'd say the chances are good he never will," Lawson said.

"Well what difference does it make now? What's done is done."

"You're right. But I'd still like to talk to someone who's evaluated him."

Davenport didn't immediately respond, instead taking a step back as he sized up his adversary, wondering what she was up to. He knew she had something in mind she wasn't sharing. Even though Lawson was now in charge of Smith's file, he still wanted to be in the loop of what was happening. Davenport sat again as he considered her request.

"What exactly is it you're hoping to find?" Davenport asked.

"I want to see what type of mind frame he thinks Smith has."

"Well what difference would it make?"

"You said it yourself. We'll only find him when he wants to be found," Lawson said.

"And the significance to that is?"

"I'm sure a man like him still has connections, sources, he's still got his eyes and ears open as to what we're doing."

"Undoubtedly."

"So maybe we get the word out we're looking for him. That we wanna talk."

"Talk? Talk about what?"

"Correcting wrongs. Making things right again," Lawson said.

Davenport took a few seconds to analyze her words and think them over, concluding she was crazy. He snapped up straight in his chair and leaned forward to get his point across.

"Are you seriously considering what I think you are?" Davenport asked. "Because it sounds to me like you're thinking about bringing him back in."

"Maybe. Now you understand why I wanna see and talk to the evaluator."

"You're crazy if you think Smith's ever gonna come walking through my door and work for us again."

"Well, he'd never do it for you. For someone else, maybe."

"That's just... that's..."

Lawson wasn't really interested in any of his objections though, cutting him off before he could finish whatever it was he had an issue with. "I don't really care what your thoughts are on the matter, Mr. Davenport. For the record, you've had three years to either find him or close the issue entirely. You've failed on both counts. Now, unfortunately, it's up to me to clean up the mess you created. Quite frankly, one which never should've been created to begin with. So now, are you going to give me the information I'm requesting? Or should I go over your head and call Director Roberts to get what I want?"

Davenport leaned back in his chair, a little agitated at the woman standing in front of him, taking over his case. He knew as much as he resisted though, he couldn't really fight it. This was all orchestrated by Director Roberts and Davenport knew that if Lawson wanted it, she'd get it. Director Roberts was the one who wanted this and appointed her so Davenport knew he didn't have a leg to stand on no matter what it was he objected to. Even though it was against his better judgment, Davenport lifted the phone and called down to the psych evaluator.

"Brian, I'm sending someone down to see you," Davenport said. "She wants to get information on a couple of agents. 17 and John Smith. Director Roberts has tasked her with finding Smith so give her whatever she needs."

Davenport hung up and locked eyes with Lawson, neither of them saying a word for a minute. The Centurion director did not look the least bit pleased at having to take orders from her, believing that she didn't have a clue what she was doing.

"Thank you," Lawson said.

"You can thank me when you're finally done here."

Lawson smiled, not at all upset at Davenport not seeming to enjoy her company. "So where can I find this guy?"

"Brian Bernier. Office 508, fifth floor."

Lawson quickly turned around and stormed out of the office and headed for the elevator. As soon as she got out on the fifth floor, she could immediately tell this floor was less hectic. It was actually kind of eerie how quiet it was. As she looked up and down the hall, she didn't notice one person roaming around. The walls were painted a dark gray, the carpeting was dark, everything seemed so devoid of life. It was a complete deviation from what she found on the sixth floor, where everything seemed bright and modern. Even the lighting on the fifth floor seemed sparse, not to mention there wasn't one door or office you could see into from the outside. They were all closed off to wandering eyes. There were no glass offices or doors on this floor. In reality, the fifth floor was used exclusively for testing purposes, as well as physical and mental evaluations. It was a floor nobody ever really wanted to visit. And nobody would unless they were ordered to do so. Lawson quickly found office 508 and slowly pushed the door open, unsure what to expect. She was almost immediately greeted by a man sitting at a desk. He was an elderly man, looked slightly overweight, probably in his mid-sixties, with gray hair and glasses.

"You must be Sam Davenport's protégé," the man said.

"Well, I doubt he'd put it quite that way," Lawson said. "I'm sure he'd call me a few other things first."

The man laughed. "I'm Brian Bernier, the psych evaluator here. Sit, please."

"Thank you. My name's Michelle Lawson."

"A pleasure. I understand you're looking for information on 17 and John Smith."

"Yes. Mostly on Smith, though."

"What exactly would you like to know?" Bernier said.

"Well I've read all the reports, the ones they've written, the ones written on them, their assignments, everything. But to find Smith, I guess I'm hoping to find out what makes him tick."

"Well, 17 was a very good agent. He was confident, maybe overly so at times, a bit cocky, had a definite mean streak in him. But he always got the job done. Loved his work. Maybe too much."

"And Smith?"

"Very driven. He wanted to be the best. Professional, set in his ways, somewhat of a loner," Bernier said.

"Are you aware of what became of the both of them?" Lawson asked.

"Well I know 17 was killed in an airport in Ohio and Smith disappeared after he was scheduled to be terminated, if that's what you're inferring."

"Were you consulted before the order was given on Smith?"

Bernier didn't answer at first, instead taking a second to collect his thoughts and determining what he was willing to reveal. Lawson could tell he was beginning to hedge a little and sought to alleviate any concerns he might have had.

"I'm not here to get anyone in trouble," Lawson said. "I've been tasked by Director Roberts with finding the man who killed 17 and with finding John Smith. They may well be one and the same thing. Anything you tell me will not leave this room and anything you say will not be held or used against you in any way."

Sensing a trustworthy person sitting in front of him, Bernier finally relented and decided not to hold anything back. "I was not consulted on the Smith action."

"Are you aware of the circumstances that led to the decision?"

"They believed he became a security risk, I was told."

"And what do you think?"

Bernier once again didn't reply immediately. The strain on his face told Lawson he was hesitant to relay his true feelings on the matter. "It's not my job to make those decisions."

"It's not what I asked, doctor. In your opinion, was John Smith a security risk?" Lawson asked.

"In my opinion, no. He was not."

"Why did you believe he wasn't?"

"As I said, he was a driven man. But from my experience, agents who turn against their country are usually driven by three things: money, power, and revenge. None of those things would have described John Smith at the time."

"What did describe him?"

"Like I said, he was driven by his need to help people, help his country. Money didn't motivate him. He wasn't interested in power. And there was nothing in his life he felt the need to get revenge for."

"Did you know about his girlfriend?" Lawson asked.

"We talked about it once. He felt conflicted about his relationship with her."

"How so?"

"It was a new experience for him. His entire adult life he'd been a loner. He went from a military unit to government work, never really having any time to devote to another person. He wasn't sure he could continue having a relationship and do the job he did. He wasn't sure he could turn the switch off from violent killer to loving boyfriend then back again. He wasn't sure he could love someone, or have someone love him, while he did the things he did. He viewed himself as somewhat of a monster, someone not deserving of another's affection."

"And yet he considered leaving for her?"

"She made him feel like a normal person, like he wasn't the things he thought himself to be. The longer he was with her, the more he liked it, the more he thought he could be something else," Bernier said.

"After his girlfriend was killed, do you think he would've sought revenge on the man who did it?"

"If you're asking whether he would've sought the man responsible, then yes. He wouldn't think of it as revenge though."

"How would he look at it then?"

"He's a man who lives on principles, on his own code of conduct. He follows his own rules. He's a man who protects those who can't protect themselves. He's got a strong sense of justice. He would look at it as righting a wrong, bringing the man responsible to justice."

"That would explain it then," Lawson said to herself.

"Explain what?"

"If Smith killed 17, it would explain why he never went after anyone else who was involved. He didn't go after his handler, or anyone else he perceived to be in on it."

"Because he's not interested in revenge, per se," Bernier said. "He's mostly interested in righting wrongs, protecting others, then he is on extracting retribution. He understands the business he's in, the life he leads, that sometimes he's going to be in danger and have to defend himself. Sometimes against people he might trust. He doesn't view those others as anything other than doing what killers do. Killing an innocent civilian, though, in his mind, would be reprehensible."

"So, revealing secrets or classified information isn't something you think he'd do?"

"Not in his DNA. He told his girlfriend he worked on

a secret government project he wasn't at liberty to discuss further. She never pressed him on it."

"And even with her gone and after what was done to him, he'd never go back on that?" Lawson said.

"It's been what, three years? If he hasn't done it by now, he never will."

"If he's found, do you think he could be brought back in?"

"What an interesting proposition," Bernier said. "Under the right circumstances, yes. He's still never betrayed his country, even after almost being eliminated, and his girlfriend killed. It wouldn't be easy though. It'd have to be the right person asking. As you can imagine, he wouldn't be very trusting of many people right about now."

"But you do think it's possible?"

"If you appeal to his sense of morals and he feels he can trust you, then yes, I do think it's possible."

"Where do you think a man like him would wind up after all this time?" Lawson asked.

"Hmm... interesting question. I would imagine he would hide out for a little while, lay low, try to stay out of sight for a while. But it wouldn't be for long. A man like him has a strong sense of morality, doing what's right, protecting people. I'd imagine, even if he wanted to stay hidden, he'd be drawn out by his perception of helping others. He has an unbelievable set of skills and he'd want to use them."

"Small town or a big city?"

"I would think he'd choose a big city. Plenty of opportunity to do what he does without the fear of being recognized."

"Really? You don't think he'd choose a smaller city for that purpose?"

"No. When you think about it, if he does the things he's capable of, and he unleashes the beast inside him, if he does it in a smaller town, he's going to stand out."

"But in a bigger city he can blend in," Lawson said.

"Exactly."

"Any ideas as to what city he'd choose?"

"I would say somewhere along the east coast," Bernier said.

"Why the east coast?"

"It's what he's familiar with. Centurion's in New York, his girlfriend was in Florida, if he killed 17, he was in Ohio. See the pattern?"

"Why wouldn't he go to the west coast, or even leave the country? Why would he stay here? Wouldn't he think it's more dangerous for him?"

"I don't believe he even considers the danger factor. I don't think he's concerned about being found. He's the type who believes if someone's looking for him, they'll eventually find him, wherever he may be."

"Do you think he'd be alone? Would he have help?"

"Most likely alone. If he's not, it's a small number, maybe one or two others he'd consider trustworthy enough to not turn on him. If there are others, then they're probably also on the run from something."

"Thank you, doctor, you've been a big help."

"My pleasure."

"Just one more question. Have you ever conveyed any

of this to Davenport or anyone else involved in Centurion?" Lawson said.

"No."

"Why not?"

"They've never asked."

"Why do you think that is?"

"Honestly, I don't think they were ever too concerned about finding him," Bernier said. "As long as he was out of the picture, that's what was important to them."

"Why?"

"I think they realized what kind of mistake they made and any attempt to bring it into the forefront would make them look... not so good. Out of sight, out of mind."

"And the death of 17 brought it back into the limelight."

"It did."

"Anything else you'd like to add?"

"The few times I talked to Smith, he seemed like a good man. I wish you luck in your travels. If you're hell-bent on finding him, I'd suggest you start by looking at cities where the crime rate has gone up, specifically murders."

7

Recker had been waiting outside of the club for several hours. He was standing across the street, leaning up against the building, just watching and waiting for his intended victim to arrive. The club didn't open until nine, but Recker got there early to conduct some surveillance and just get a general feel for the area. He saw Laine walk into the club about eight o'clock. He came back out about half an hour later to start dealing with some of the crowd as the line started forming. Judging from the amount of people waiting to go in, Recker assumed it was a fairly popular place. Though the club was located in the middle of the street, there were small walkways located on both sides of the building, leading to a larger parking lot in the back of the property.

Recker patiently waited for the right time to strike. He fielded a couple of phone calls from Jones while he waited, wanting to see if he'd done the job yet. But Recker said he was waiting for the crowd to die down a little. He also saw there were security cameras on the entrance, as well as the corner of both sides of the building. Killing Laine might not be as easy as he thought it'd be. He could've just picked a spot somewhere and took a sniper shot at Laine from across the street, but somehow, it seemed like taking the easy way out to Recker. Anybody could do that. It took a special kind of person to kill someone up close. But he also felt as if avoiding the cameras was going to be a bit of a challenge. He didn't see a way he could've avoided them if he was going to do it there. But as he thought about it, he could sense he was getting overanxious and pressing. Two things he normally didn't do. He was usually very patient in waiting for one of his victims. But for some reason, he was trying to force this one. Maybe it was because he was feeling the CIA heat he was trying to hurry things along so he could get back to working out whether he was at risk. All he had to do was wait a few hours more until the club was closed. He already knew Laine's address. If he just waited until the business was closed, he could just follow Laine home and avoid the security cameras.

With his new plan, Recker went back to his car which was parked down the street. He still had a good view of the club and could see Laine's car as he was leaving. Once Laine got back to his house, Recker could finish him off with relative ease. It would likely be three or four in the morning once he got home and Recker wouldn't have to worry about prying eyes. He called Jones and informed him of the plan so he wouldn't bother asking him every half hour on whether the job was finished yet. Recker was parked in a metered spot and had to put some change in the machine every couple of hours as he waited. He thought about just going to Laine's house and waiting, but Recker didn't want to take the chance of his target going somewhere else first before stopping home. Then Recker might have to wait another day to finish his task. And though he was trying to be patient, he wasn't interested in prolonging this any further. He wanted it to be done tonight. Not only so he could get back to monitoring the CIA more closely, but also because every day Laine was alive, was a day a child could get hurt because of him.

Recker kept his eyes on Laine for most of the time, just in case he ducked out early. But he was still there come closing time at 2am. He stayed for half an hour after closing and most everyone else had left, though there were a few employees still there. Recker knew there was a back entrance and Laine would likely leave through there. Knowing he wasn't likely to see his target physically leave the building, Recker had to pay extra attention to the street where the cars exited. Luckily, there was only one exit. He finally saw headlights beaming across the side of the building, indicating a car was coming out. It was Laine's. Not wanting to get too close and possibly scare the man off if he noticed he was being followed, Recker kept a comfortable distance between the two of them. Especially at that time of the morning where there weren't a lot of cars out on the road, it'd be much easier to spot him if he followed too closely. Luckily, Laine appeared to be going straight home without any stops. It was about a twenty-minute drive from the club to Laine's home, which was located on a quiet suburban street.

As they pulled onto the street, Recker sped up, hoping to catch up with Laine before he actually entered the house. As he got closer, he could see he was a little too late, as Laine was already unlocking and opening the front door. Recker parked along the curb just as the door closed, making it a tiny bit tougher for him to enter. He honestly didn't feel like jumping through hoops for this assignment and decided to just be straightforward about it. Though he could've gotten in the house by some other means, it was always easier to just go in the front door. The tougher part would be whether or not Laine answered at that time of the morning, since it wasn't exactly normal to hear someone knocking at your door at 3am. But Recker didn't really care, he had a gun, he'd just start blasting away if he had to. Most people were sleeping anyway, and when they heard gunshots and woke up, he'd be long gone. But just to err on the side of caution, Recker put a suppressor on the end of his gun. It'd still make a sound, but it would be severely muted and not quite as noticeable. As Recker walked up the steps to the door, he thought about how he was going to finish the job. He could kill him the moment he saw him, but it wasn't Recker's style. He at least wanted the man to know in his final moments, why he was being killed. Recker didn't think he owed it to them, but he thought it was only fair. Recker loudly knocked on the door several times and waited a minute for an answer, though none was coming. He repeated his steps, only to get the same response. He noticed a doorbell and rang it continuously until he heard footsteps coming.

"All right, all right," Laine shouted from the inside. "What the hell do you want? It's 3am."

"I'm just here to take out the garbage," Recker said sarcastically.

Recker had been hiding his gun underneath his trench coat, firmly planted within his hand. He immediately withdrew it from his coat and pointed it at the unsuspecting man.

"Yo, man, whatever you want, just take it," Laine said, putting his hands up.

Recker didn't bother responding and instead pulled the trigger, shooting his victim in his left shoulder. Laine fell backwards, yelling in pain, and clutching at his shoulder as Recker entered his home.

"Yo, what do you want?" Laine asked.

"You hear what happened to your friend, Bowman?"

"I heard he was killed yesterday."

"Give you two guesses as to who did it." Recker grinned.

"Why? What do you got against us?" Laine asked, crawling backwards along the floor to try to escape his attacker.

"I don't like people who use children for their own pleasure."

"What're you talking about?"

"I know your record. I've seen the text messages you and Bowman exchanged. I know what you were planning."

"All right, man, I admit it. I promise I'll never do it again. I promise."

Recker was getting tired of walking and pursuing the man so he shot him in the thigh to stop him in his tracks. Laine screamed out in pain, wondering how long the man was going to torture him for.

"If you're gonna kill me, just get it over with," Laine said.

He was right. Recker didn't want to torture him while killing him. He usually only tortured people he had a personal vendetta against. He didn't even torture 17 much. Recker ended his life rather quickly for all the pain and anguish he'd caused him over the years. Recker did what he wanted and let Laine know why he was killing him, which was all he set out to do. He raised his suppressed gun at Laine's body and fired three more rounds into his chest, quickly snuffing out the remaining breaths of life within him. Not one to admire his work very much, Recker immediately turned around and walked out the door. As he walked to his car, he looked around to see if anybody was on the street, but there was no one to be seen. As he drove away, he called Jones to let him know the job was done. Jones had said he wouldn't go to bed until he heard from Recker when everything was finalized, no matter what time it was.

"David, it's done," Recker said.

"Any complications I should be made aware of?"

"No."

"Where did it happen?"

"Inside his house."

"And there were no witnesses, onlookers, anything?" Jones asked.

"No, it was a clean hit."

"Very well. I guess I shall see you in the morning then."

Recker drove back to his apartment, though he didn't go straight to bed. He was tired, but still somewhat wound up from the altercation with Laine. Though Recker believed he was completely justified in the killing and nobody would lose sleep over the death of a child abuser, it still wasn't something he could just forget in a matter of minutes. He never could. Even when he was in the CIA, he couldn't just block out someone dying and forget about it in a matter of minutes, and it hadn't changed since then. When he got home, he fixed himself a rum and coke and sat on the couch to take some steam off. He didn't bother to put the TV on, a light, or anything else to distract him. He just sat alone on the couch in the darkness, trying to sort out his thoughts. He finally slumped on the couch about 5am and drifted off to sleep.

It wouldn't be as long a rest as he was hoping for though. He initially didn't figure to get into the office until around noon, as was usually the case when he was out late on an assignment the night before. But he normally didn't have someone banging on his door in the morning either. Recker was awoken from his sleep by the thunderous pounding on his door. He reached for his gun which was still sitting on the table and slowly sauntered over to the door.

"Mike, I know you're in there. I saw your car outside," Mia yelled.

Recker took a look through the peephole, not believing what he was seeing. Though he obviously knew Mia's voice, he had no idea she even knew where he lived. She picked him up from the lot the one time he left his car downtown after taking out Bellomi and his crew, but he never told her which unit he was in. And he definitely wasn't expecting her right now. He took another look through the peephole, as the door shook from her knocks, just to make sure there was nobody with her. She seemed to be alone, so Recker finally opened the door for her. Mia barged in, not even waiting for an invitation.

"Sure, come in," Recker said.

Mia stormed into the room, looking like a ball of fire and like she had a lot on her mind. She put her hands on her hips and turned around to face her host. Recker looked at her curiously, wondering what was on her mind.

"What do you think you were doing yesterday?" Mia asked.

"What are you doing here?" Recker said.

"I wanted to talk to you."

"Ever hear of a phone?"

"No, a phone won't do for this. This needs to be done in person," she said, agitated.

"How'd you even find me?"

"I know where you live, I've been here before."

"No, you've been in the parking lot. I never told you what unit I was in."

"Well, you don't need to be a world class investigator like some people I know to figure it out," Mia said. "I looked at the names on the mailboxes in the lobby."

Recker let out a laugh, not believing her. "No, I took my name off the mailbox."

"Exactly. You have the only mailbox without a name attached to it. I assumed you'd be the only person who'd go that far."

"Hmm, not bad. But what if you made a mistake and pounded on the wrong door?"

"Then I guess I would've just used my sweet personality to apologize." She gave him a mock smile, crinkling the corners of her eyes.

"Oh."

Mia took a quick look around the room since it was the first time she'd actually set foot in Recker's apartment, not really impressed with his décor.

"How many years have you been here?" she said.

"Uh, a few."

"And this is all you've done with it? I've seen warehouses looking better decorated than this."

"Well I'm not here much anyway," Recker said, looking around. "All I need is the basics. Got a kitchen, a couch, a TV, a bedroom, it's everything I need. I don't need fancy pictures and china and candles and all the other nonsense. I'm basically only here to sleep."

"Speaking of which, did I wake you up? You look like crap."

"Late night," he said wearily. "What time is it, anyway?"

"After nine."

"Oh. Well, I had to get up in like three hours, anyway."

"Oh. Sorry. I just figured you were up already. I assumed you were on a case or something."

"Was. Finished it last night. Late last night."

"What time'd you get to bed?"

"I think I dozed off at four or five. Something like that anyway."

"I'm sorry," Mia said, some of her bitterness fading away.

"You want a drink or something?"

"No. No. You almost made me forget what I came here for. You probably did it deliberately. Change the subject, make me feel sorry for you so I forget all about it."

Recker grinned and shrugged. "Not me. I would never."

"Yeah right."

"Don't you have work today?"

"No, I'm actually off for a day."

"Lucky you. Well, why don't you run along and spend time with your new BF," Recker said, grabbing her arm and leading her to the door.

Mia quickly shook off his grasp of her and took a few steps back, getting the urge to fight again, ready to light into him.

"No. You know how mad I am at you for yesterday?" Mia asked.

"Yesterday? What was yesterday?"

"Are you seriously gonna pretend like you don't remember what happened?"

"Refresh my memory. I barely know what day I'm in half the time. With my schedule, all the days just blend together sometimes," Recker said, playing dumb, though he knew exactly what she was referring to, buying some time so he could fashion a sarcastic reply.

"You know, lunch at the hospital, you, me, Josh. You remember, that one?"

"Oh," Recker said, tilting his head back, changing his voice slightly as he played along. "Yeah. I remember now."

"Yeah, I thought you might."

"What about it? What are you mad for? I thought we all had a great time."

Mia laughed. "Great time? Yeah right. You know how embarrassed I was sitting, listening to you?"

"Why? I thought we were all just sitting there, talking, trying to get to know each other."

"No. I know exactly what you were doing. It was the very reason why I didn't want to introduce you yet."

"Why?"

"Why? Because you were trying to make him look bad, you were trying to intimidate him, you were trying to..."

"I meant no harm," Recker said gently.

"You really think I believe that?"

"Well, I mean, he kind of seems like a... like a..."

"Like what?" Mia said, hands on hips.

"Like a tool."

"Seriously?"

"Just my opinion. I think you can do better than him."

"No. You're not playing this game with me."

"What game?"

"You're not doing this. You don't get to choose who I

go out with. I was never so embarrassed as I was yesterday listening to you."

"Really? More embarrassing than being kidnapped and tied up in an empty office with a psychopath and a notorious gang and your life hanging in the balance?" Recker asked.

"That wasn't embarrassing. That was just... it was... I dunno, it was just something else." Mia stammered the words, caught off balance.

"Oh. Makes sense."

"You're gonna need to ease up on him."

"Does it really matter? It's not like I'm gonna be seeing the guy every week."

"Well, if we're still gonna be friends, then you're gonna need to get used to seeing another guy around me."

"Mia, all kidding aside, if it makes you uncomfortable being around me from now on, I'll understand. If this other relationship is something you really want, then try to make it work the best you can. If there's not room for me, I'll be OK."

"I don't want to cut you from my life. I don't. I understand things between us will never progress the way I once hoped. I'm accepting the situation. I am. But I still care about you, and I don't want to never see you again. I know we're never gonna go double dating or anything sappy, but there's no reason we can't still see each other from time to time."

Recker nodded, agreeing with her position. "OK. I promise I'll never try to intimidate him or embarrass you or anything."

"Besides, you still need me. Who else would you go to if you ever got shot again? Which is probably likely considering everything you do." Mia's lips curled up slowly into a tight smile.

"Good point. Maybe I'd just have to find myself another nurse."

"You better not."

"OK. I promise I'll be on my best behavior next time."

"That's all I ask."

New York---Lawson entered the Centurion offices with vigor, confident she was on the right track in finding her target. Well, maybe it was more hopefulness than confidence, but regardless of semantics, she felt like she was making headway. She felt that she had a good understanding of her subjects, how they thought, how they behaved, and where Smith might have gone. She went into Davenport's office to request a few things that she needed.

"Mr. Davenport," Lawson said.

"Mr. Davenport's in conference right now," the secretary said without looking up.

"Well, you can either buzz him to come out or I can start pounding on his door."

"Uh, just one minute."

The secretary called into the office and told Davenport that Lawson was here and insisted on seeing him immediately. Within a minute, Davenport opened the door and emerged from his office, closing it behind him as he greeted Lawson.

"I hope this is important," Davenport said. "I have critical business that I need to get back to discussing."

"I have important business that I need to discuss too," Lawson said, standing her ground.

"What do you need?"

"I need two of your analysts assigned to me for the next couple of days."

"Why?"

"I believe John Smith may be in a major city somewhere on the east coast. I need a couple of analysts to try to track him down."

"What makes you think he would be on the east coast?" Davenport asked, sounding unconvinced of her findings.

"Well, after talking to the doctor, along with my own personal observations, that's the conclusion we've come to," Lawson said.

"Sounds like a wild goose chase to me."

"Somehow, you don't surprise me."

"Fine. I'll have two analysts report to your office within half an hour."

"I'll be waiting."

Lawson then left to go back to her office while Davenport stayed stationary, thinking about whether she was as close as she believed she was and who he wanted to send to her. He then turned to his secretary before heading back to his meeting.

"Have Fulton and Rogers report to her office immediately," Davenport said.

Approximately twenty minutes later, the two analysts came to her office as she was working on her laptop.

"Ms. Lawson?" Fulton asked. "We were told to report to you."

They exchanged pleasantries and the two analysts told her about themselves. After talking to them for a few minutes and picking their brain a little, Lawson was satisfied she was getting good people she could work with. She explained the situation to them and what she was looking for.

"I would like you to start combing through airport surveillance footage," Lawson said to Fulton. "I want you to pay specific attention to two dates. The date we know Smith flew back into the country, and at the Bob Hope Airport where 17 was killed. I want you to also check out flight manifests for every flight into the country the day he was supposed to fly in."

"OK."

"Rogers, I want you to start digging into records and information for every major city on the east coast."

"What do you consider major?" Rogers asked.

"Boston, Philadelphia, New York, Atlanta, Washington, DC., Miami. Start with those first then work your way down if nothing comes of them."

"What exactly am I looking for?"

"Statistics for major crime increases in the last three years. News stories of a new gang or player in town, police requests for information regarding an individual where they don't have much,. If Smith has relocated into one of these cities, it's likely murders or major crime stats have probably gone up, and it's also likely the local police have nothing on him and have attempted to gain insight into his identity by requesting further information, either from us or the FBI."

"I'm on it."

"Thank you both. With some luck and hard work, hopefully we can pinpoint his location within a few days."

8

The Philadelphia Police Department had called a 10am press conference to discuss a string of recent murders plaguing the city. All the major news organizations were there, TV stations, newspapers, and news blogs, basically anyone who had press credentials. Though it wasn't being broadcast live on TV, the stations were just cutting up footage and highlights for their later news broadcasts; it was being streamed live on their websites. Ever since the day before when the police announced they were holding a news conference, Jones started looking into it and had a feeling that him and more specifically Recker would be the main topic. Well, more or less all Recker since he was the face of their operation. Both he and Recker were in the office watching the live stream of the event on the computer. Police Commissioner Paul Boyle stepped up to the microphone to start the conference.

"Thank you all for coming. The reason for this conference is to discuss several murders that have happened in our city recently. The last two having occurred in the past three days. We believe the deaths of Sidney Bowman and Reed Laine is the work of the man that the media and the public have dubbed The Silencer. We are releasing a picture of the man that we believe to be The Silencer and are hereby announcing him as wanted in connection with their murders. We are asking for the public's help in identifying this man so we can prevent any other incidents from happening. If you know who this man is, where he lives, or you see him walking down the street, please call the police tip line."

Boyle stepped aside as a picture of Recker appeared on a screen behind the commissioner. It appeared to be a picture from some type of security camera from the shopping center where Recker left the car and body of Sidney Bowman. It was a still shot of Recker walking away from the car. Jones glanced over at Recker, who returned his look with a shrug.

"I didn't see any cameras," Recker said.

"Obviously," Jones said. "This isn't going to help matters any."

Boyle talked about the deaths of the two men, as well as several other incidents reported to be the work of The Silencer over the past several years. He recounted not only murders, but also other minor cases they thought Recker had been involved in. After Boyle had finished his speech, he opened the floor to questions from the media.

"What makes you think the man is The Silencer?" a reporter questioned.

"This is the first actual photograph that we've gotten

of him that matched up with some of the sketches that have been drawn over the past few years."

"If The Silencer did do these, what makes you think it was murder and not self-defense?"

"We have evidence that would indicate murder. I can't really get into further specifics than that."

"Doesn't Laine have a long police record?" another reporter asked.

"A man's criminal history has no bearing on whether his murder is investigated or not," Boyle said.

"Yes, but, with all due respect, every instance that you've reputed to be the work of The Silencer, innocent people have been protected, and criminals have wound up either in jail or dead."

"As I said, a victim's criminal history has no bearing on anything. The Silencer is not a member of law enforcement and is not entitled to just go shooting people at will. This isn't the wild west. We have law, we have courts, we have a justice system. We do not work outside of those controls just because we feel like it and call it justice. It's not how it works."

"But you're asking for the public's help on something they don't want to help you on," the reporter said. "I've talked to several citizens who think The Silencer is more helpful than the police are."

"Well that would be false and incorrect."

"But the public perception is, he helps the weak, the vulnerable, and the innocent. And the only people who get hurt are the criminals who are trying to capitalize or prey on them. The public supports him and believes he does what should be done and what's necessary, or does what the justice system fails to do."

"I can't help the public perception. All I can state is he's not a police officer, and he does not have justification for some of the things he does," Boyle said. "He must be held accountable the same as anyone else. It's the law."

Commissioner Boyle took a few more questions, none of which were very sympathetic to his cause of capturing or identifying who The Silencer was. As the reporters' questions indicated, the media, as well as the public, were firmly behind The Silencer. It wasn't very likely the police were going to get the kind of support they were hoping for. As the conference started to wrap up, Jones started wondering about their future.

"Should we begin packing?" he asked.

"I don't think that'll be necessary."

"Well your profile just went up five thousand percent."

"From a police standpoint, this is nothing new. I've always been on their radar. They've sent up requests to the FBI before. They're just making it public now."

"Why now after all this time?"

"I'm making them look bad I guess," Recker shrugged.

"Still, this won't make our jobs any easier."

"Wasn't easy to begin with."

"Well this won't help."

"They're grasping at straws. They're not likely to get much help from the public."

"That's a very premature assumption to make I would say," Jones said. "Your picture was just released by the police to the public and will likely be plastered on every bulletin board, bus stop, website, train station, and blog site known to mankind."

"Hate to break it to you but my face hasn't exactly been a secret for a long time," Recker said. "They've had sketches of me from almost every case I've been on since we started. From the girl I saved from getting raped at the bar, the woman I saved from her husband at the hotel, or the convenience store I saved from being robbed, they've always known what I looked like. Now they just have a physical picture."

"Still, I can't believe this won't somehow reach the ears of the CIA. This has to reach their doorstep somehow," Jones said.

"Maybe."

"For the sake of simplicity, it may be better if we start up operations in another city."

"You really wanna pick up and move?" Recker asked.

"Do I want to? No. But in the interest of self-preservation, I think it may be wise. We've always known this day may come. We always knew there could be a time when the heat became too much and it would simply be more difficult to work here. Perhaps the time has come. We've talked about this."

"I know. I just don't know if I wanna keep doing this every few years. Moving."

"Why?"

"I dunno. I feel like we've established something here," Recker said, rehashing the same conversation they had earlier.

"We've never really put down roots," Jones said.

"There's nothing to prevent us from going somewhere else. Pack up the computers, load up a moving van, and we're gone. Just like that. There are other people in other cities who could use our help, just like this one."

"I know. It's just... I'd hate to lose all our contacts, friends, and have to start all over again."

"To be fair and honest, we only have one friend. And she's moving on, Mike. She's got a new relationship, she won't be around as much, there's really nothing keeping you here. You can make contacts in other places just as easily as you did here."

Recker nodded, knowing he was correct. "Yeah. Let's give it a couple weeks first and see what happens. If it looks like it's getting too hot, then we'll pack it up."

"Deal."

"Have you picked up anything in the last couple days on the CIA front?" Recker asked.

"No. It's been quiet."

New York---Lawson was in her office working on some leads when Rogers came rushing in, a little out of breath. He had his laptop in hand and set it down on Lawson's desk and started typing on it.

"You're not gonna believe this," Rogers said calmly, although the speed of his entry and the glint in his eyes gave away his excitement.

He pulled up the picture of Recker off the Philadelphia Police Department's website from the photo they released of him from the press conference they had the day before. Rogers zoomed in on the picture and blew it up across the screen to get an even better look at it.

"Oh my god, it's him!" Lawson said.

"Yeah, that's what I thought."

"Where'd you get this?"

"The Philadelphia Police Department released the picture yesterday."

"Why? What happened so he'd be on their radar?"

"They're linking this man to a couple of murders that happened there within the last few days," Rogers said.

"Who were the guys he supposedly killed?"

"A couple of nobody's. One was a convicted child sex abuser, the other was a friend of his, might've dipped his toes in the same pool, just not caught yet."

"This is the break we've been looking for."

"Maybe. If the heat's on him then he might just pick up and leave," Rogers said. "Might be gone by now, anyway."

"OK. We stop everything else and concentrate on Philly," Lawson said. "We know he's there. So, let's put the pieces together and figure out what he's doing there and who he's doing it with. I'll contact the Philly police and see if I can get a look at the file they have on him."

"You got it."

Lawson immediately got on the phone and called the Philadelphia Police Department. After talking to a couple different people and being put on hold for a few minutes, she eventually was put through to Commissioner Boyle. After a quick greeting and identifying herself, she quickly got to the heart of the matter.

"I understand yesterday you held a news conference

and released a picture of a suspect in some murders you've had recently," Lawson said.

"Yes, that's right."

"I believe we can help you in that regard if you're willing to reciprocate that help."

"What did you have in mind?" Boyle asked.

"We know who the man in the photo is."

"Who is he?"

"Well, first, before we get into that, I'd like to set some ground rules."

"Such as?"

"Well, I'd like to look at the file you have on him, everything you suspect him of."

"That could be arranged," Boyle said.

"Great."

"How is it that you know this guy?"

"I can't really divulge that, sir."

"C'mon, you're gonna have to do better than that. You want my cooperation? Fine. I'm willing to give it. But cooperation is a two-way street and if you want my help, then you need to fill in the dots."

"OK. I'll tell you what I can," Lawson said. "He's a former CIA agent who, due to various circumstances, is no longer with the agency."

"He went into business for himself?"

"Maybe. Kind of looks that way. There's some debate amongst some of us as to what to do with him."

"Oh, you got that too, huh?"

"What's that?"

"He's been here about three years as far as we can

tell," Boyle said. "At least that's when we first started getting reports on him."

"Yeah?"

"Well, you'll see when you read his file, but so far, he's only targeted criminals. He helps the elderly, stops robberies, kills the thugs... he's a one-man task force."

"So, what's the debate?" Lawson said.

"You know how many people I pissed off in my own department with the press conference yesterday?"

"No. I guess I don't quite understand the problem."

"The problem is half my command, eighty percent of my patrol units, and sixty percent of my detectives want to leave the guy alone and let him do his thing," Boyle said. "They say he makes their job easier. They wanted me not to release anything and possibly scare the guy off and have him go to a new city."

"So, why'd you do it then?"

"Like I said in the presser, nobody's above the law. Even those who apparently are on our side. Sometimes, people trip over their halo if it falls off."

"I get your meaning."

"What's this guy's name?"

"John Smith," Lawson said.

"Really?"

"No, it really was his name with us. I don't know what he's using now."

"So, what are you guys planning on doing with him?" Boyle said.

"Well, it'll largely be up to him, assuming I get close enough to talk to him."

"You wanna talk to him?"

"Absolutely. He has a special set of skills which could be useful."

"You don't have to tell me about that. I've seen his work."

"Anyway, I can be down there tomorrow morning if that works for you," Lawson said.

"Yeah, fine."

"Can I ask one other favor of you?"

"You can ask."

"I know you just put it out there and he's your number one target, but can I ask you to back off it already?"

"Back off?" Boyle asked, surprised at the request. "You're telling me how dangerous he is, not that I need a reminder, and you want me to back off?"

"He's been missing for three years," Lawson said. "I don't want to take the chance of him feeling the walls are closing in so he flies the coop and we lose track of him again for another three years. This is the closest we've gotten to him. I don't wanna lose him now. I'm just asking, please, you don't actively pursue any leads on him until we get a team down there."

"Well, I'm not going to make any promises right now. The media and the public love his persona, so I don't even know if we're going to get any leads that are worth pursuing. I'll take it under advisement."

"Very well. I'll be down tomorrow morning."

When Lawson put down the phone, she could hardly contain her excitement. After only a few days of searching, she'd already got a line on Smith's whereabouts. It made her wonder how she could find him in a few days when the previous regime couldn't find him in three years. Then she thought about what Bernier told her and how they didn't seem to be looking for him very hard. She believed Davenport knew he'd made a colossal mistake in trying to terminate Smith and the easiest thing to do was just to sweep it under the rug. Keeping it at the forefront only reinforced what a grave error he'd made. Regardless of Davenport's reasons or ineptitude, this would be a big feather in Lawson's cap. Though she wasn't initially too sure about this assignment, she was beginning to warm up to it. She kind of liked the idea of working on specialized cases and being the big gun, brought in to save the day. Now, she just had to deliver. It was one thing to find Smith. It was another to take him out or bring him in.

Davenport was in the outside office with his secretary discussing his itinerary for the next couple of days when he noticed some activity going on in the hallways. He saw both Fulton and Rogers, analysts that he had assigned to Lawson, fly by as if they had some urgent news to share. Wondering if they'd found something, Davenport eagerly left his office and swiftly walked to Lawson's to see what the fuss was about. When he got there, Lawson and the two analysts were almost giddy and going over plans of some kind.

"From your demeanor, I take it you've caught a break," Davenport said.

"Not just a break," Lawson said. "We've found him."

"What? You found him?"

"Yes. I wish I could say it was our brilliant deductive

skills, but I can't. Philadelphia police released a photo of a murder suspect."

Lawson pulled the picture up on her laptop and spun it around so Davenport could see.

"That's him," he said softly, a little stunned.

"Yes, so I'm heading down there tomorrow to talk with their police commissioner and see what they've got on him so far," Lawson said. "Maybe I can get a read on his behavior and pinpoint where we might find him."

"And your goal is to what? Take him out, have a conversation with him, what?"

"I'd like a chance to talk to him first."

It was not the answer Davenport wanted to hear. A displeased look came over his face, still believing taking Smith out was the only option. Mostly because it would look bad on him to bring back an agent who he tried to eliminate. He was worried. If Smith was brought back, Davenport would look even worse in the eyes of his superiors, and who knows, maybe even get demoted, or lose control of the Centurion Project. He wasn't about to take a chance and let that happen.

"Can we have the room, please?" Davenport asked the analysts.

Fulton and Rogers looked to Lawson, knowing there was about to be a major disagreement. Since they knew she was technically in charge of the assignment at the moment, they wanted to clear it with her first. She nodded at them to do as he asked and the two analysts went back to their own workstations.

"What exactly do you think you're doing?" Davenport asked tersely.

"I think we've already had this discussion before. I'm cleaning up your mess."

"I know what you're doing. You think if you can somehow bring Smith in you'll be a conquering hero, the white knight, or the cowboy riding into town, saving the girl, then rides back out the next day in a blaze of glory. It doesn't always work so easy."

"Why exactly are you afraid of me trying to bring him back?" Lawson said. "Afraid of how it's gonna affect your reputation? Or maybe, you'll have to answer more questions from the higher-ups on why you seemingly gave up looking for him? Or is it something else?"

"None of the above. I'm just trying to help you. I know this assignment is a big step up for you and you're being looked at for future promotions," Davenport said. "I'd hate to think you blew your big chance on some wishful thinking or some grand delusion you may have."

"So, you're just looking out for me?"

"Men like Smith cannot be rehabilitated or brought back or reconditioned. His trust is broken. Whether that's our fault isn't relevant. You want to play the good guy and make it seem like you can do something nobody else could."

"And your point?" Lawson asked, not believing a word he was saying.

"You need to be realistic. If you get close enough to talk to Smith, then you're close enough for him to put a bullet in your head. And that's the most likely scenario. If he even gets so much as a sniff of one of us nearby, his first action isn't going to be waving at you, or asking how you're doing. His first action is going to be trying to put a bullet between your eyes. And you might want to think about that possibility."

Davenport turned and left her office to go back to his as he contemplated his next move. Though Lawson knew most of what Davenport was telling her was fluff, there was one thing he said which did make sense. It was how she was going to get close enough to talk to Smith. He was right, Smith would come up shooting as soon as he knew the CIA was near him. Though she'd eventually have to figure out the answer to a tricky question, the more pressing concern was just finding him to begin with. Once Davenport got back to his office, he immediately gave his secretary a new task.

"I want you to give me a list of the closest available agents we have who are not currently on assignment," Davenport said.

"When do you need it by?"

"Within the hour. Drop everything else and get me those names as soon as possible. I may need one of them for a very urgent job."

"I'll get right on it."

Davenport went into his office and tried to get some work done, though he quickly gave up on trying to do anything. No matter what he tried to do, his mind wound up thinking about Lawson and Smith. Knowing that Lawson wasn't going to abandon her attempt in trying to recruit Smith once again back into the organization, Davenport was hellbent on making sure she wasn't successful. Whatever it took, he was going to make sure she failed. His secretary got back to him half an hour later, bringing a list of names into his office and setting them down on his desk.

"We have two agents here in New York," she said before leaving.

"Perfect. Thank you."

Once his secretary left, Davenport perused the list a little more closely. It not only had the names of the ten closest agents, it also mentioned their strengths and weaknesses in a little spreadsheet. After looking at it for a few minutes, Davenport selected the agent he thought was best suited for the job and called his number.

"Agent 23, I have a new assignment for you. It's completely off the books, there won't be a record of it anywhere," Davenport said.

"What is it?"

"You're getting two targets. I'm sending a picture of each of them to your email," he said, bringing up the pictures of Smith and Lawson on his computer screen.

"What do you want done with them?"

"Eliminate them. Both of them."

"Where will I find them?"

"Philadelphia. I want you to be there by the morning," Davenport said. "I want you to stay there until the job is done. I don't care how long it takes."

"Does it matter who gets it first?"

"Take Smith out first. He's the more dangerous of the two. Once he's out of the way, she won't be much trouble."

9

As she promised, Lawson drove down to Philadelphia the following morning and was accompanied by three other agents. It was a little after 9am, and her first stop was police department headquarters. Commissioner Boyle cleared a few minutes from his busy schedule to accommodate the CIA officials. He was under no obligation to work with them, since they had no official capacity within the United States, but he figured if he did them a favor, there might come a time when he could seek a return on the favor. It may have been wishful thinking since the CIA was extremely guarded with their information no matter who the inquisitor was, but Boyle figured it was worth the chance. Joining the commissioner in his meeting with his guests from the CIA was Deputy Commissioner Devron King, Boyle's right-hand man.

After a brief introduction and some small talk, Boyle handed Lawson the file they'd accumulated on Smith, the man Philadelphia knew as The Silencer.

Lawson eagerly read the contents of the file, trying to gain any insight she could into how he was picking his victims or what part of the city Smith was likely to be found in. She had short bursts of conversation with her guests as she read the file, trying not to get too distracted so it would make her lose focus on what she was reading.

"Just from what I'm seeing, there doesn't appear to be any similarities to any of these cases which would seem like they're related in any way," Lawson said, frustrated there wasn't an obvious lead to be had.

"Now you see the problem we've been facing for the past several years," Boyle said. "He leaves behind no traces, no evidence of any kind, nothing helpful to us."

"Then how do you attribute all these cases to him?"

"Witnesses at the scene," King said. "All the people interviewed at the scenes of these crimes described seeing the same man, similar build, same type of clothing. It's why we're fairly certain everything in this folder is his work. Stopping rape victims, robberies, possible murders, assaults, you name it, he's been there."

"How do you account for how he's been at the scene just before these crimes have happened?" Lawson said.

"We can't." Boyle shook his head. "We just don't know."

"There has to be a way he's getting there ahead of time. It can't just be luck."

"We agree. We just haven't figured out how he's doing it yet."

"He must have help," Lawson said. "He can't be working alone. There has got to be another guy. Or girl. I mean, someone has to be feeding him this information somehow."

"The only thing we can come up with is he's got some kind of underground network informing him of impending crimes. How it works exactly, we have no idea."

"Any idea of who he might be working with? He can't be doing this all himself."

King threw his arms up, indicating their lack of knowledge on the subject. "It's a little perplexing. The fact all his targets are criminals, it's kind of strange if he'd be working with other criminals to make it happen."

"Maybe whoever he's working with isn't a criminal. At least not in the way we'd view them. Looking through these cases, it doesn't seem like he sticks to any one area specifically."

"He's been all over this city," Boyle said. "Northeast, south, west, downtown, there isn't an inch of this city he hasn't covered."

"Have you gotten any tips worth acting on since you went public the other day?" Lawson said, trying to flesh out the little information she had to go on.

"Nothing worth mentioning," King said. "At least not concerning him."

"What do you mean?" Lawson asked.

"Well, over the past few years where we can definitely pinpoint he's been here, the number of anonymous tips we've received has tripled. Not necessarily about The Silencer, but about crimes in general. And many of them have been preemptive in nature."

"That's a little strange. How do you account for it?"

"We can't. We don't know how it's related, or even if it's related at all. It's just kind of an interesting sidebar."

"I have to admit our main goal in having the press conference wasn't exactly getting any type of information leading to his capture or anything," Boyle said. "We didn't expect anything of that nature to come from it."

"Then what was the reason behind it?"

"Our chief principle behind it was to bring him out into the light. A man like him works in the shadows. Our goal was to hopefully shine some light on him so his profile is raised to the point where it's uncomfortable for him to work here. Hopefully, he'd pick up and leave and go on to a new city."

"So, you have no expectations of help from the media and the public?"

"I think I explained to you yesterday about the debate The Silencer has caused within my own department," the commissioner said.

"Yes."

"Well, double that with the media and the public," Boyle said. "They view him as a modern-day Wyatt Earp, riding into town, cleaning it up, killing all the bad guys by whatever means necessary. The public will be absolutely no help. They love the guy. They view him as doing what the police won't do."

"Media too?"

"He's regular headlines for them. They wouldn't like to see him go away anytime soon. He helps sell papers. They cater to what the public wants. While there's a few who don't agree with his frontier style of justice, there's just as many if not more who agree that he's more adept at taking out the trash than we are."

"Has he ever targeted an innocent person that you can tell?" Lawson asked.

"As far as we can tell, he's never hurt anyone who did not have a criminal record," Boyle said. "And we're not talking criminal records as minor as jaywalking or loitering or something. He targets hardened criminals, those with murder, assault, armed robbery, crimes against children, against the elderly, gang bangers, you name it, he's nailed them."

"What about these last two you think he killed? I thought one of them had no record."

"He didn't. But we found incriminating text messages on his phone he'd exchanged with the other guy indicating he had some severe mental issues. He didn't have a record yet, but it looks like he was heading that way. He just hadn't been caught in the act."

"I can see why your department is split on him," Lawson said.

"Split is a bit of an exaggeration," King said. "There's probably more who view him as an asset and appreciate all the help he gives us as opposed to those who think otherwise. He's a very polarizing subject amongst us, as well as the entire city. Look, there's no doubt, while this guy's been here, crime has gone up. But there's also no doubt the number of dangerous criminals on the street have gone down. In saying that, while this guy appears to know his craft, and appears to be on our side, he's also sprung up a bunch of wannabes. Guys who don't really have any idea what they're doing."

"You mean copycats?"

"Exactly. There's been at least ten people we've identified as being disciples of his, not that he's endorsed them, but who apparently idolize him and what he seems to stand for."

"It's bound to happen," Lawson said.

"No doubt. But these copycats are dangerous. Half of them don't have the skills to do what he does and wind up dead themselves. The others are too dangerous to have a gun in their hands and target just about anything that moves, good, bad, or indifferent. So, it's not necessarily just him that's the problem. It's everything he represents. If it was just him, maybe we wouldn't be having this discussion today. But you just can't have a bunch of people running around the streets extracting their own brand of justice," King said, he seemed exasperated at the whole situation.

"Now, we've been very forthcoming and honest with you in regard to what we know and what we have," Boyle said. "I'd appreciate some honesty in return as to how you know this man as well as anything else you can tell us. Legally, you're not even supposed to be here, so you technically can't even operate within this city without someone in my department leading the charge."

"OK. I can't tell you everything," Lawson said. "But I'll tell you what I can."

"I'd appreciate it."

"I don't know what name he's using now, but when he worked for us, he used John Smith. That's what he's known as."

Boyle rolled his eyes, knowing it wasn't likely to be the man's real name either.

"He worked in foreign intelligence in secret black ops projects which required certain skills," Lawson said, continuing the briefing.

"I can imagine what those skills were," Boyle said.

"Something happened, something went wrong, something that shouldn't have, and he himself was targeted based on false information. He dropped off the grid and has been missing ever since."

"And what made him pick here to set up business?"

"We have no idea. I just took over the investigation to find him within the past week. I got information indicating he may have been in a major city on the east coast, then one of my analysts caught wind of your press conference and saw the picture you released of him, and here we are."

"So, what exactly do you presume on doing?" the commissioner said.

"Well, as you said, we can't legally act here without your knowledge and consent," Lawson said. "But you obviously have a problem on your hands regarding him and we believe we can help you with it. With your permission, we'd like to stay here indefinitely and conduct operations with the intention of finding him."

"And when you find him?"

"I would like to take him into custody and transport him back to one of our facilities."

"And what if he doesn't want to go?"

"Well, hopefully it won't come to that."

Boyle sat back in his seat, leaning against the brown

leather lined chair, thinking about his options. He looked up at his deputy commissioner as he thought.

"How long do you intend to stay here?"

"However long it takes. Hopefully a few days, maybe a few weeks," Lawson said. "But if we need to stay longer, we will. We're not leaving here without him. Unless we have evidence he's gone somewhere else, in which case we'll obviously follow him."

"I'll give you permission and authority to stay and work here under one condition."

"Which is?"

"I need updates every day from you about your operations. I don't want any of my officers walking into a potential war zone because you found him, cornered him, and neglected to inform," Boyle said.

"I can agree to that."

"Would you need any further help from me?"

"No, I don't think so. If we could get a copy of these files, it's about the only thing we really need. It'll help in trying to map things out."

Boyle handed the file to his deputy commissioner and said to make a copy of everything in it to help the government agents in their quest.

"One last thing, it's kind of interesting. Not only have crimes gone up, but also way more preemptive tips have come in. Do you think there's a correlation there?" Lawson said.

Boyle threw his hands up. "Who knows? We haven't ruled it out but we have nothing to indicate it's related. Why would it be?"

"Well, if he's only targeted the so-called bad guys, and

he gets wind of crimes about to happen and he can't get there, perhaps he phones it in."

"Well the increase isn't on the phone hotline," Boyle said. "It's anonymous emails coming through our system. It's skyrocketed."

"Any chance you tried to trace where those emails came from?"

"Well, the tips are routinely analyzed and matched against IP addresses from any prior messages, just to make sure we're not getting fake tips from the same address all the time."

"I take it you got nothing from them?"

"Well, some IP addresses show up a few times, but that's to be expected if it's from a higher crime neighborhood, or someone who's extra vigilant. But nothing extraordinary. So, if he's part of the increased volume of tips, we don't have any evidence to implicate him."

"Hmm. Well it was just a thought."

"Well if that's all we can do for you then I wish you luck and hopefully a quick resolution." Boyle reached out to shake hands.

Lawson reciprocated the handshake and her team left the commissioner's office, ready to embark on their mission. After getting a copy of Smith's folder, their first move was to check into a hotel and set up their operations and begin to go over plans. Based on the information in the folder, Lawson wanted to map out every location they believed Smith had ever been. They hoped, once they had done it, maybe they could discern some type of pattern leading to a consensus on his base of operations, or where he was likely to be.

It was late afternoon, and Recker walked into the office with a box of pizza for dinner. It'd been a relatively quiet couple of days since the police department's release of his picture. For his part, Recker didn't really change his behavior much. He didn't go into hiding or only go out at night time. He didn't cling to the sides of buildings or wear a hat down over his eyes. He walked around much the same as he usually did. The only difference was they had no cases to work on. Jones kept telling him things were on the horizon, he just had to flesh out the details a little more, but Recker started to get the feeling he was stalling. He had the idea Jones was flustered by the increased activity surrounding them, both with the police and the CIA, and he was putting cases off they should've been working. Once Recker put the pizza on the table and the two men began eating, he started quizzing his friend on his suspicions.

"Seems awfully strange we haven't had any cases in the last couple days," Recker said.

"Yes, well, it happens. We've had lulls before."

"Just seems a little coincidental when it happens right after a major police news conference where they release my picture."

"Indeed," Jones said.

"Or right after we learn the CIA has put me back on their radar."

"Quite a coincidence indeed."

"David, you wouldn't be intentionally hiding cases from me, would you?"

Jones laughed, though Recker could tell a disingenuous laugh from him every time. "Don't be ridiculous."

"When things seem to get a little hot for us, you have a tendency to shut the door for a while and try to hide away," Recker said.

"Well it's a good thing one of us does. Maybe I worry too much, but you don't seem to worry enough."

"It's not that I don't worry or I'm not concerned. But I know you can't change how you act. You could hide away for a month, then the very first day you step outside, they nab you. Then what good was the month of hiding?"

"I'm not sure your analogy is valid," Jones said.

"Sure it is. You can be as careful as humanly possible and do everything you can to avoid what's coming, but it doesn't mean you can."

"So, what do you suggest? Do nothing."

"No. I suggest we do what we've been doing. Act normal. We go about our day just like always and do what you signed me up for. It doesn't mean we ignore any dangers. We'll keep monitoring them, and if something comes up which makes us have to deviate from our plans, we act accordingly. But no mass hysteria," Recker said calmly.

Jones sighed deeply, knowing his friend was probably right. He was overreacting. Jones tended to overcompensate when it looked like trouble was brewing. He was just very cautious and always preferred to err in that direction. After they finished eating, Jones finally admitted he had been intentionally pushing cases off to the side they could have been working on. It was nothing extremely urgent, such as an impending murder, or someone's life in jeopardy. If that was the case, then Jones surely would have acted upon it more swiftly.

"Well so long as it's settled, how about we look and see what's on the agenda?" Recker asked.

"Very well."

Jones walked around the desk, sat at his computer and began typing away to bring up the necessary information for Recker's next assignment. Pictures of four men came up on the screen.

"Who are these clowns?" Recker asked sarcastically.

"These clowns as you put it, appear to be a very dangerous crew."

"Crew? You mean literally?"

"Yes. It would appear they are a crew in every essence of the word," Jones said. "They've all got lengthy records and each of them are considered violent. Their last arrest was six years ago for an armed robbery of a restaurant. They were apprehended and arrested a few minutes after the event."

"So, what are they planning this time?"

"Looks like a jewelry heist," Jones said.

"Where and when?"

"David's Jewelry Store."

"Oh. Have another business you been hiding from me?" Recker cracked a joke.

Jones didn't crack a smile. "Don't be silly."

"Where is this place at?"

"On seventeenth street."

"When are they hitting?"

"The store closes at nine. The crew indicated they'd hit tonight close to closing time when there's not so many people," Jones said, checking his notes.

"How'd you get wind of it?"

"My software program picked up a set of text messages from a couple members of the group where they were talking about 'robbing them blind', as they put it. I started digging up the background info on the phone numbers, then everything just fell into place from there."

"How long ago?" Recker said.

"A few days."

"What were you gonna do if I didn't press you on this? Just let the place get robbed?"

"Of course not. I was planning on doing something," Jones said. "I just hadn't figured out what yet. Maybe send an anonymous tip to the police or something."

"Yeah, 'cause we haven't done that too much," Recker said, rolling his eyes. "You know, can they trace all those anonymous emails back to you somehow?"

"Seriously? Bite your tongue." Jones smiled. "Who do you think you're talking to? Of course they can't trace them back to me. Do you think this is the first time I've done this or something?"

"Well I just figured I'd ask. It's a cinch the CIA will be checking into it."

"No. Every anonymous email is automatically assigned a different IP address. If they check into it, they'll come up as various places throughout the city. And some outside the city I might add."

"Just thought I'd ask."

With some time to kill before the jewelry store heist, Recker and Jones went back to work for a little while. But after a few minutes, Recker remembered something he'd been meaning to bring up with his coworker. It wasn't a big deal, and with the other things on their plate the last couple of days, it didn't rate high on the priority list, but Recker did wonder about it.

"You know, it's kind of funny," Recker said.

"What is?"

"I had lunch with Mia the other day and you didn't ask anything about it."

"What's to ask? People have lunch every day," Jones said plainly, though he knew what his friend was insinuating.

"I don't."

"Well you're not normal."

"I also don't meet new boyfriends every day either."

Jones stopped typing away at the computer and pushed his seat away as he started coughing, at first forcing it before it actually became necessary.

"You alright there?" Recker asked.

"Oh yes. Just a... you know, something caught in the old pipe there."

"Shame you couldn't have been there."

"Yeah, well, you know."

"So how long were you keeping that secret from me?" Recker said.

"I wasn't keeping secrets from you."

"So, you didn't know she had a boyfriend?"

"Well, I, uh, might have heard something to that effect. But I was not keeping a secret."

"Then what would you call it?"

"I was just not sharing... news which wasn't mine to tell," Jones said, stumbling over the words.

"Wait, was it the secret meeting you had and you wouldn't tell me about?"

"Umm, possibly."

"Uh, huh."

"She merely wanted to ask my advice on how best to approach the subject with you."

"Because you're such a relationship expert?"

Jones shrugged. "When it comes to matters of the heart, I'm purely Switzerland. I'm neutral and not getting involved."

"Since when?"

"Since always."

"Yeah, OK."

"So, are you saying you actually met Mia's new boyfriend?" Jones asked.

"I did."

"Well it's a surprise she introduced you already."

Recker smiled. "Yeah, came as a surprise to her too," he said with a laugh.

"Wait, you met him by accident?"

"Apparently the guy canceled lunch, then Mia called me. Then the guy freed himself up and came over to surprise her."

"And she was surprised?"

"You have no idea."

"And though I have my own guess as to how the luncheon went, how was it according to you?" Jones said.

"I thought it went fine."

"And for them?"

"Well, I think I was a lot to take in the first time meeting me."

"You are a bit of an acquired taste," Jones said. "You

have a certain disposition that may be off-putting to some people."

"So I've been told."

"And Mia was fine?"

"No, she was terrified," Recker said truthfully.

"I can imagine. I'm sure you did your best to make it as awkward as possible."

"I did not."

"Maybe one day I'll get Mia's version of the events."

"I think she's trying to burn the memory of them."

"I bet. Anyway, what did you think of her boyfriend? What was your impression of him?" Jones asked.

"I didn't like him."

"Why doesn't it surprise me?"

"No, it's not what you think. It's not because I don't want to see her with anyone else or I'm jealous or anything," Recker said.

"Then what was it?"

"I just plain didn't like the guy."

"Why?"

Recker grimaced, trying to think of the reasons behind his dislike for Mia's new boyfriend and properly explain them without sounding like a jealous ex-boyfriend. And it truly was just a general dislike for the guy. In his profession, he usually had to make quick decisions about trusting people in tight spots or high-pressure situations, and he considered himself to be a pretty good judge of character. Sometimes, first impressions were all he got from people. So, he was an experienced hand at sizing people up at first glance.

"I dunno. He just doesn't seem right for her," Recker said.

"Very astute observation," Jones said sarcastically.

"I'm not jealous. I don't have the right to be."

"Well I agree there."

"No, it's just... something seems off about him. Just personality wise."

"Does he seem shady?"

"Well, he is a lawyer," Recker said, laughing. "No, joking aside, it's not that. He might very well be a decent guy."

"I'm sure we'll find out in time."

"I think I got it," Recker said, continuing to think about it. "You know what it is? They didn't seem like they gelled. They didn't seem like they had any chemistry together."

"Well I'm sure it was awkward with having you there in the picture."

"Maybe."

"You're enough to spoil anyone's chemistry."

10

Recker had stationed himself a little way down the street from the jewelry store, just sitting in his car and watching the place for a while. He got there around seven, wanting to make sure he was there in plenty of time so he could stake the area out before the impending robbers arrived. Recker thought for a while as to how he wanted to handle the situation. He and Jones debated it for close to an hour before Recker left the office, not coming to a definite conclusion on the best way to diffuse the dangerous situation. No matter what he did, there were pluses and minuses to it. Recker figured he had two options, and both had a set of difficulties. The first option was to let them do the job and try to pick the gang off as they came out of the store. The problem with that would be if the shooting started early, and the gang got split off or separated, some of them might get away. It would mean Recker would likely have to deal with them again soon. His first choice was to eliminate them all at one time. The other problem with a shootout outside the store was that some of the gang might retreat inside if they couldn't reach their getaway car in time. It might lead to a hostage situation with whoever was working inside the store or any customers who were still left shopping.

The second option they considered was, Recker would go inside the store sometime before closing. In that scenario, he'd already be in there waiting for the crew. The danger there would be that everyone who was inside the store would be put in harm's way. Now, he could've handled it as he had in other instances, and walk inside and let the workers know what was about to go down, and take their place and wait himself. But he also figured it wasn't likely all four men would go inside to do the job. It wasn't a huge jewelry store and didn't need all four men of the crew going inside. Recker assumed at least two would go in, maybe three. Maybe the fourth would stand outside the door and be a lookout. Or if two went in, maybe one would be outside as the lookout and one would stay in their car, ready to squeal out of there in a hurry.

There was no easy answer. In every scenario Recker dreamed up, there was just as good a reason he could think of as to why he should go in a different direction. If it was just some inexperienced run-of-the-mill gang that wasn't dangerous, Recker might not have put as much thought into it as he was. He could've handled it no matter which way he chose to go. But these guys, this crew was experienced in this type of work. They'd done it before and done it well. Plus, they were known to be violent. These weren't some young kids Recker could intimidate or get the drop on because they didn't know what they were doing. This crew would likely shoot first at the earliest sign of trouble or if something didn't appear to be right or going according to plan.

After giving it ample thought and going over every different scenario he could think of, Recker finally came to a conclusion as to how to handle the situation. With how experienced this crew was, he thought it was best to wait outside for them. If he could be sure all four men would make their way inside the store, then Recker would've preferred to already be in there waiting. He could get everyone to safety first, then take his chances with the gang. But he just didn't believe more than three would walk in. In fact, the more he thought about it, the more he believed only two would go in. He tried to think of how he would handle it if he was the one robbing the store. In that case, since it wasn't a big store, and it was near closing so they wouldn't have to handle a ton of customers, Recker would only take one other person in. He'd leave one man at the door to prevent anyone from coming in, or take the chance someone would walk by and see what was going on, and he'd leave one man in the car as the driver so they could fly out of the area in a jiffy. Another problem was, Recker couldn't identify them before they actually walked into the store. They weren't likely to use any of their own vehicles, and whatever car they did use, would most likely be stolen, so he wouldn't be able to see them in advance.

It was situations like these where he wondered if it was time for a partner in the field, someone else who could handle themselves the way he could. If there was, one of them could've waited inside and dealt with whichever crew members came inside, while the other could take care of the ones on the outside. It was never something he seriously contemplated or something he even put a lot of thought into when it did cross his mind, but now he was, he wondered if it was something he should bring up with Jones. Especially with the CIA hot on their trail or more specifically, his trail. Jones really had nothing to fear from them. They didn't have anything on him. Recker was the one they were after. And though he always tried to put on a brave face and pretend he wasn't worried, he was concerned, partly about himself and partly about Jones. He worried about what would happen to him if Recker was gone. Though he suspected Jones would eventually carry on without him, it would take him some time to get things right again. With them being together the past several years, they had everything down to a science. They knew each other well and knew what each other was thinking, what they would do, in virtually every situation. If Recker was no longer there, Jones would have to find a replacement, then slowly integrate them into the business, then develop a trusting relationship, just to get back to the point they were at now. That would take years. And though it could be done, there would be a lot of people in the meantime who wouldn't get the help they could've and should've gotten.

After a few more minutes of contemplating, Recker shrugged those thoughts from his mind and got back to his current problem. If he was going to take out the entire gang after they robbed the store, he had to figure out how to take out the first two without alerting the members inside. He wasn't sure it could be done discreetly. Unless he could take them all out before going inside. That would present a whole distinct set of problems. Instead of dividing them to make the numbers smaller, he'd be taking them all on at once. But if he did it that way, it wouldn't endanger any innocent people on the inside and they certainly wouldn't be expecting it. Recker looked at the time and knew he had to stop waffling on a decision and stick to a plan. To pull this off, he was going to have to be fully committed to whatever it was he decided. Knowing time was running short, he finally decided to stick to his original plan. He'd take out whoever was left on the outside, then get the others as they came out the door. He'd have to make it work. From his vantage point, he had a good view of the front of the store, so he'd be able to easily see when the crew arrived.

As the time drew closer, Recker knew it was almost time for action. It was 8:45pm. The crew would be arriving any minute. He was well prepared in terms of firearms, as he had taken three weapons with him. He had one Glock in his hand, one in his belt, and an assault rifle strapped to his back, plus a few extra clips. If a fire-fight erupted, he'd be ready for it. Recker got out of his car and walked over to the other side of it, stretching his legs and getting himself ready. All the while, he kept an eye on the jewelry store so he had an idea of how many customers were inside. After ten more minutes, the crew still wasn't there yet. Although it was possible, they decided to scrap their plans, Recker still believed they'd show up. They still had five minutes, and he figured they were waiting as long as possible. Just a few seconds later a black van slowly drove past him, finding a parking spot a little up the street, not quite level with the jewelry store. Right after parking, three men spilled out of the van and ran toward the store. Recker instantly recognized the crew from the photos they had of them.

As the men approached the store, they put black ski masks on before they entered. Somewhat surprisingly, all three men entered the store. Recker assumed one of the men was standing on the inside of the door to prevent surprises and whoever was left in the van was guarding the street. Whatever the case, it made it a little easier for Recker. He knew time was short, and he had to make his first move now. Knowing the man inside the van was probably looking through the mirrors to make sure nobody came up from behind, Recker walked in the street by the cars. He got out his keys and fumbled with them in his hand to make it look like he was walking toward his car. With the van just a few feet in front of him, he put his keys back in his pocket and replaced them with a gun. As he got near the van, he could see through the side mirror that someone was still in the driver's seat. Still walking toward it, as he reached the tail-lights, the driver rolled his window down. Recker cautiously approached the door, knowing there was a chance the driver was waiting for him with a weapon of his own. A few inches from the door, Recker saw the left hand of the driver reach out and set it on the edge of the rolled-down window.

Once Recker got to within reach of the door, he pulled on the handle and opened the door, causing the driver to slightly lose balance. Even though the driver was waiting for him, he wasn't expecting the stranger to open the door on him. The two seconds that caused the driver to lose his balance was all Recker needed to gain the advantage. As the driver tried to steady himself and raise his own gun he had in hand, Recker pointed his weapon at the man and fired twice at point blank range. Two shots lodged firmly into the man's chest meant the crew just lost their getaway driver. Recker, while keeping one eye on the store, reached into the van and pulled out the keys from the ignition. He turned and tossed them into the middle of the street then went back towards the rear of the van. He peered around the edge, keeping his eyes centered on the entrance of the store. He thought about maneuvering a little closer to the store but wasn't sure if he'd have time before the robbers came out of the store. He didn't want to get caught out in the open without having some type of cover. At least where he was, he had the van for protection. They would be heading there anyway, so he figured it was best just to wait there.

Two minutes later, the three remaining members of the crew came rushing out of the store, two of them carrying a black duffel bag, presumably holding whatever jewelry, cash, and other valuables they had just pilfered. The three men planned to stagger their positioning to avoid being grouped together, with the first man getting to the truck, then the second man, then the third. As the first man got to the curb, Recker jumped out from behind the van and unloaded on the unsuspecting robber. Three shots into his chest knocked the man onto his back then Recker turned his attention to the next man who was halfway between the store and the getaway vehicle. Recker fired at the second guy, also hitting him several times in the chest and midsection. With the first two men down, he fired at the third guy, who retreated toward the store entrance. As he took another shot at the man toward the store, Recker was shocked to see the first two guys stumble back to their feet. Recker knew he hit both of them square and was stunned they weren't dead yet. As they returned fire from their respective locations, Recker took cover behind the van.

"Crap," Recker whispered to himself. "Must be wearing vests. Wasn't counting on that."

Recker put his Glock in its holster and grabbed the assault rifle from his back and spun it around to a firing position. He figured if they were wearing bullet-proof vests than he needed a little more firepower. With a few bullets from his targets glancing off the van or lodging into its metal exterior, Recker dropped down to the ground and fired his rifle at the first member of the crew. Instead of aiming at his chest, Recker fired at the man's legs, chopping him down to size as he fell to the pavement, bullets ripping into his shins. The second member of the crew started to run back toward the store entrance as well, but Recker quickly fired before he could get there, hitting the man in the back of his thighs as he crumpled to the concrete walkway. Recker looked for the third member of the crew but he was nowhere in sight. He must've retreated into the store. With the first two members of the crew seemingly down and out, Recker stood and came out from behind the van into the open. He swung the rifle onto his back again and pulled out his Glock as he walked toward the injured men on the ground. Seeing an assault rifle was still on the ground within reach of the pain riddled man, Recker kicked his gun away from him. As he stood over the fallen robber, the man could see what his shooter's intentions were.

"Please, man," the man said, holding his legs in pain.

"Today's not your day," Recker said.

Recker unloaded one round into the man's head then moved to the next member of the gang. The man was still lying face down as he was grabbing the back of his legs. The man was screaming in agony with his legs feeling like they were on fire. As Recker passed over the man on his way to the store, he didn't bother speaking to him, or letting him know what was coming. He nonchalantly fired a round into the back of the man's head, instantly silencing the man's screams of pain. Although it briefly occurred to him to just leave the two bullet-ridden bodies behind, alive, as he went after the last remaining member of the crew. He quickly dismissed the idea. These men were too unscrupulous, too violent, too much of a danger to society. Recker wouldn't lose any sleep dispatching these people to their afterlife. Once he got to the door, he tried to push it open, but it wouldn't budge. It appeared to be locked. He knew there was a good chance he was going to take some fire the minute he busted through the door. Before going in, Recker put in a new clip for his gun to make sure he was fully loaded. Sirens started wailing in the background. The police were coming. Recker figured he didn't have very long until they got there. A couple minutes at most. The smart move would've been to hike his way out of there before the cops arrived. But Recker knew there were still three people in the store who were now likely hostages, including the person who worked there and two customers. The police were qualified to handle hostage negotiations, but Recker thought if he left, there was a chance the guy might just kill one or two of them before the police got there. But once he did get inside, he didn't have a lot of time to get the job done. And he wouldn't have time to negotiate either. He thought he had maybe two or three minutes max to kill the guy and get out of there before the police swarmed the building.

The door was made of glass, making it unnecessary to have to kick it open. Recker grabbed his assault rifle and forcefully smashed it through the glass. It instantly smashed into tiny pieces as the small particles of glass fell to the ground. Gunfire erupted as the lone remaining member of the gang opened fire toward the door when the glass smashed. Recker took a small step back, knowing he was going to have to make his way inside rather quickly. Surprise was probably his best way to make entry. He saw a small kiosk near the front of the door he could take cover behind until he saw where his target was located. He dove through the newly opened door, again drawing some gunfire, and scurried along the light blue carpeted floor until he reached the kiosk. He sat on the floor with his back against the bottom of the wooden kiosk, taking a second to catch his breath and figure out what to do from there. The top of the kiosk was jewelry encased in glass, but only temporarily, as the case was immediately smashed to pieces as gunfire ripped through it. Recker put his arms over his head and ducked to protect his face from getting cut from the falling pieces of glass.

"Give it up," Recker yelled. "All your buddies are dead."

"Yeah, well, I ain't joining them," the man shouted back.

Recker took a quick look around to try to find the two customers and store worker to make sure they were safe and out of the line of fire. He couldn't initially find them though. He turned around and got on his hands and knees as he looked around the edge of the kiosk. He saw his target behind the main counter, though only the top of his head, as he was ducking behind it. Half a minute later, the man rose fully behind the counter, showing the rest of his body. Recker didn't fire though. The man was yanking at the hair of one of the customers, putting her body in front of his and holding a gun to the side of her head. She was a middle-aged woman, in her mid to late forties, and looked scared as could be. This was one of the things Recker had feared. He knew this scenario might come into play if he couldn't have gotten them all outside the store. Of course, he knew if he had waited for them inside the store, a whole other set of problems may have occurred. But still, he hated seeing an innocent person come into the dangerous crosshairs of the two sides. Recker also rose above the kiosk and stepped away from it, slowly walking toward the counter at his target and the hostage. He aimed his gun at the man the entire time he moved closer to him.

"Let her go," Recker said.

"Yeah, right," the man said. "She's my insurance policy. She's not going anywhere."

"You got nowhere to go. I already disabled your vehicle out there so you'd have to escape on foot. Once SWAT gets here, you know there's no escape. Just make it easy on yourself."

"As long as I got leverage, I have a way of getting out of here."

"The cops are coming, they're not making any deals," Recker said.

"Unless they want bodies in here, they'll deal."

"That's not happening. Because no bodies are gonna pile up in here as long as I'm breathing."

"Well I guess I'll just have to do something about that, won't I?"

Though Recker never took his eyes off the target in front of him, he let his ears take in what was outside, listening to the sounds of the police sirens. They weren't far off. If he didn't get out of there soon, there was a chance he was going to wind up getting trapped in there himself. He knew what he had to do. He just had to make sure he had a clean shot. He had to wait until the man made his head completely visible behind the woman's face. Though Recker was an expert marksman, he didn't want to take chances with only half of the man's head as a target.

"Tell you what, why don't we switch places?" Recker asked. "Let go of the woman and take me instead."

The man laughed at the silliness of the suggestion. "Yeah right. I ain't letting go of her. Maybe if you drop your gun first, I'll think about it."

"Think of it. Having a cop as a hostage is a lot more valuable to you than these people."

"You're a cop?"

"Of course I am. Why else would I be in here? What, you think I go around getting in shootouts for kicks?"

"Where's your badge?"

"I'm undercover. I don't carry one," Recker said.

"Throw down your gun or I'll kill this woman right here."

"I wouldn't do that."

"I don't care what you would do."

With the sirens getting louder and likely getting there within the minute, Recker knew he had to make some hay, and he had to make it now. He had to come up with a new plan.

"How about this? I'll throw my gun down, then you release the woman. Then I'll give you the keys to my car and you can get out of here?" Recker said.

"Why would you do that?"

"Cause my only concern right now is saving the life of everyone in here. And I'd rather see you get away than put anyone's life in jeopardy with a police standoff."

"I dunno, man."

"C'mon, we don't have long to debate this. Listen to the sirens. The rest of the squad's right up the street and closing in fast. If you wanna get out of here, this is your ticket. You're not likely to get another chance at this."

"You're trying to pull something on me."

"I'm not trying to pull anything. I just don't want any bloodshed and I can see what's gonna happen here if you don't take this. But if you don't leave now, you'll never make it to my car in time," Recker said.

Sweat was pouring off the man's head as he contemplated the deal. Something was gnawing at him telling him something wasn't right, but in his current predicament, he really couldn't afford to be too choosy. He knew the likelihood of him getting out of the situation as is was low. As soon as the rest of the police rolled in, he knew he was going to be arrested or killed. As Recker suggested, this was his only shot at getting out of there in one piece.

"Fine. Throw your gun down," the man said finally.

Recker did as they agreed upon and gently tossed his gun down on the ground. Before making a move, he waited until the man let go of the woman hostage. As the woman slowly slid away from her captor, the man turned his attention to Recker and pointed his gun at him as he waited for him to complete his end of the deal.

"The keys?" the man said.

"I'm gonna reach inside my pocket and toss them over to you, OK?"

"Just do it slowly."

"I don't have any other weapons on me," Recker said, lying to the man. "Just the one I already put down, so take it easy."

Recker slowly moved his arm inside his coat and reached for the handle of his backup weapon. He put his left arm up to try to keep the man at ease and not tip him off that he was about to give him a surprise.

"All right, I'm just bringing out my keys now," Recker said. "I'll toss them over to you."

Seeing the man relax his gun arm ever so slightly as

his elbow bent, Recker quickly withdrew his gun from its holster. As fast as possible, he immediately pointed it at the unsuspecting robber, who was caught a little off guard. Though the man still wasn't sure he trusted the cop's proposition, Recker's speed was something he wasn't quite prepared for. Assuming the man was wearing a bullet-proof vest like his comrades, Recker didn't bother aiming for his chest. He didn't want to take the chance in case the guy returned fire at him. Like the other members of the crew, Recker sought to finish the man off and put an end to this standoff by taking him out with a head shot. With one quick flash, Recker withdrew his gun, pointed it at the man's head, and fired, all before the man could get a shot off himself. Recker's aim was right on target as the bullet went right through the man's forehead, though not quite on center as it caught the man a little to the left. Still, it got the job done as the man slumped to the ground and died even before the impact of hitting the carpet. With the screams of the two women customers in the store not believing what just happened, the situation was now resolved.

"Everyone all right?" Recker asked.

He got either an affirmative reply or a nod of the head from the three people who remained, still a little shaken by the events. Recker looked back toward the front door and saw the red and blue lights flashing, as well as the blaring sirens. The standoff took too long. There was no escaping now. At least not the way he came in. He quickly backtracked behind the main counter and checked on the man he just killed, just to make sure there was no mistake.

"Do you need us to stay here and get statements from us?" one of the women customers asked.

"I'm not the police."

"What? I thought you said..."

"I said what I needed to say to try to diffuse the situation," Recker said.

"Well if you're not the police, then who are you?" the store worker asked

Recker sighed as he looked around for an exit strategy. "I guess you could call me a concerned third party."

"You're not here to rob us or anything either, are you?" the woman hostage asked.

"No."

Recker continued to look around, unsure how he was getting out of this one. Several things crossed his mind, none of which had a high probability of working. He could've tossed his guns away and asked the others not to reveal his role in the shootings and pretend he was just a customer there as well, but he didn't have faith the others would keep quiet on his involvement in the killings. Not that he could blame them, he just couldn't expect them to lie about something as big as this. He could've just run out the front door and started shooting, but it wasn't a very sensible option either. He wasn't too keen at shooting at the police, even if it was to save his own hide. For one, engaging the police was likely to be a suicide mission, considering there were probably half a dozen cars out there or on their way. But the bigger reason was, he didn't want to hurt any of them. Everything he'd done since he arrived in this city was to help people, protect the innocent. The police had the same objectives. They just went about their goals in two different ways. So essentially, they were on the same side. And if Recker was going down, he decided he wasn't taking any of them with him. He didn't figure they deserved to be on the receiving end of one of his bullets. He had to find another way.

"Are we free to leave?" the woman hostage asked.

"Just give me a minute to figure something out," Recker said.

The store worker was closely studying Recker's face and could tell by his nervous demeanor he was worried about the police outside. Seeing the man wasn't a threat to them, and seeing how he did help them and save them from being harmed and robbed, the elderly gentleman tried to find out what his problem was.

"What exactly are you afraid of, son?" the sixty-year-old man said.

Recker looked at the man and winced, not really sure it was a good idea to reveal anything to him and get him involved. But without any other good options, and with time running short, he gave a deep sigh and figured it was worth a shot or a last-ditch effort.

"Well, I'm not a so-called bad guy. I'm on the side of the good and the innocent," Recker said. "But the police and I have extremely different ways of going about the way we protect people."

"So, they'd likely lock you up, huh?"

"And throw away the key most likely."

"That's a predicament, isn't it?"

"You heard of the guy who has been running around the city the last few years? The Silencer?" Recker asked.

"The guy who goes around helping people and getting rid of thugs and criminals?"

"Yeah."

"Yeah, I've heard of him," the gentleman said.

"Well, you're looking at him."

"You're The Silencer?"

"Yes, sir, I am."

"Can we go yet?" the woman customer asked, tired of waiting for their conversation to end.

"Just hold it a cotton-picking minute," the worker said.

Recker smiled at him, thinking he seemed like an all right kind of guy.

"Hold on, we'll get you out of here, son," the worker said.

"Now I'm not going to do anything which will put you in danger, even if it means me having to stay here and take my lumps with the police," Recker said.

"No, no. Come with me. You ladies stay right there for a second," the worker said.

The elderly man led Recker into the back storeroom and to an exit door leading to the rear of the building where the trash dumpster was kept. As they walked, the police were yelling into the store via a megaphone to see what the situation was, not knowing whether any of the would-be robbers were still inside, or how much of a danger it was. Recker was about to push the door open and see what the situation was out there until the store worker stopped him.

"Just hold up there, young fella," he said. "There's an alarm box on the side here. If I don't disarm it and put the code in, there's gonna be a loud, obnoxious sound that'll be heard around the block."

The elderly man walked over to the alarm box and put the code in to disarm the door, then Recker gently pushed it open just a hair, looking out into the alley behind the store. Recker was disappointed, but not surprised, to see there were police cars lined up at both ends of the block. They would cut off his escape route and throw his plan out the window. He closed the door again, and the man put the code back in to arm the door once again. Thinking there was nothing else to do but give himself up and take his chances with the law, the store worker had one more idea to try. The man looked up at the ceiling and put his hand on Recker's forearm to stop him from going back to the front of the store.

"There's your only hope now," the man said, pointing to a ladder on the wall leading up to the circular roof hatch.

"Where's it go?" Recker said.

"Just up to the roof. The only people who use it are roofers, or the heating and air conditioning people."

"Guess it's as good a shot as any."

"Hold on, let me disarm the alarm again."

Recker scurried over to the wall and started climbing the ladder. He got about halfway up before he stopped and looked down at the elderly man.

"Hey, thanks for the help," Recker said, appreciative of the man's efforts in aiding his escape.

"No problem. Keep on what you're doing. And thanks for the assist out there."

"I'll keep a special eye out for you."

Recker continued his climb up the ladder and pushed the roof hatch open. If it'd been a little later than it was, he might've been concerned about SWAT team snipers picking him off once he got up there, but even if they'd been called, they didn't have enough time to get there already and set up. Once Recker stood on the roof and looked around, it was actually a perfect scenario. As he stood there, he wasn't visible from the street, as the edges of the store walls extended up past the rooftop, creating some cover for Recker's movements. Each store on the street had connecting walls to the business next to it so Recker quickly climbed over the wall onto the roof of the next store. He wasn't sure how far he'd have to go, or how he'd get down, but for now, it seemed like a good escape.

The jewelry store worker waited three or four minutes until him and the two female customers made their way outside into the waiting arms of the police. He figured it was what Recker needed to slip away. Once the police swept the store and started questioning everybody and figured out what happened, Recker would be long gone. Recker wasn't really concerned with anyone knowing he was there, anyway. Once Recker got to the end of the block, he used some piping, gutters, and ledges to climb himself down the side of the building. The police didn't block off the entire back alley since it'd be too long an area to partition, and instead only blocked off a few stores down from the jewelry store in both directions. Recker walked around to the front of the building and started walking back up the street to get in his car. But there was heavy police activity all around and they weren't too far from his vehicle, so he figured it was best to leave it for the time being. The last thing he needed now was to be spotted and get into a police pursuit. He'd have to come back for it another time. He called Jones to let him know the task was completed, and he needed a ride out of there.

"What was the score?" Jones said.

"Good guys four, bad guys nothing," Recker said.

11

Lawson and her team were up early to discuss their different options on finding Recker. They got started right around 6am as they gathered in one of the hotel rooms. Lawson's phone rang only a few minutes later to inform her of the details of the jewelry store incident from the night before. It was Deputy Commissioner King who told her of the incident, hoping it could maybe help them in their search for the wanted man. After a brief conversation with her counterpart, Lawson thanked him for the information then got back to her team and started brainstorming. She explained to them what happened at the jewelry store as it was explained to her.

"OK, so he's obviously getting some inside intel somehow," Lawson said. "How is he figuring out how these crimes are going to happen? He's there ahead of time, waiting for the criminals to get there. He's obviously got something in place. Some kind of system."

"Here's a far out, off the wall theory," one of her assistants said. "What if he sets up these crimes, recruits criminals to pull the job off, then stops it before it happens or just after it happens so he looks like the knight in shining armor?"

"It's an awful lot of trouble to go through without getting anything in return," Lawson said. "I mean, he's not getting money or anything from this stuff."

"He's getting notoriety. Maybe that's what he wants."

"You don't disappear from the CIA just to go to a big city and build up a reputation," Lawson said. "No, notoriety is the last thing he wants. Besides, it doesn't fit his profile. He's a low-key guy. He's not after fame or fortune. I think he genuinely is trying to do good things."

Another of Lawson's assistants chimed in with his thoughts. "Well, if it's not the notoriety, which I think we all can agree it's probably not, then we need to focus on how he's getting this information. What if all these people he's stopping are part of the same underground criminal network? They have a leader who dispatches them on these jobs and Smith has a beat on them, maybe an informant who spills what they know to him."

Lawson thought it over for a minute, but by the grimace on her face, wasn't sold on the idea. "I don't know, I have a hard time believing every crime he's stopped is from the same network. I mean, don't you think after a few times they would've shored things up if they felt there was a leak?"

"Yeah, probably."

"If the group had any brains, after the third or fourth time, they would've completely dismantled their system."

"True. That leaves only one other possibility then."

"Which is?" Lawson asked.

"He's getting the information straight from these criminals. It's not like these people are going on message boards on the internet and declaring publicly what crimes they're gonna do. He's somehow getting into their phones, their computers, their emails, something telling him what's going on."

Lawson paraded around the room as she thought. She not only believed it was as good a theory as they were going to come up with, she actually thought it might not be too far from the truth.

"OK, so let's say that's the case," Lawson said, looking around her team. "He still needs to find a way to do it. There's nothing in his background that suggests he could do something like this on his own. It can only mean he has help."

"Not only that, but it'd have to be a sophisticated system," one of the analysts said. "Unless he's just got a list of criminals and getting into their computers remotely, he'd have to come up with something very technologically advanced to pull this information out of the air."

"But you think it is possible?"

"Sure. If he's found a way to hack into the infrastructure of say... emails, for example, he could have certain words or phrases plucked out and send him an alert, or maybe even a copy of the email."

"It would require a lot of time to create a system like that," Lawson said.

"Maybe. Maybe not."

"What do you mean?"

"Well, if we do assume he's not in this alone, then it's possible his partner, or partners, are computer whizzes. Maybe, they take care of the information gathering, sorting it out, Smith goes out in the street and does what needs to be done."

"Possible."

"In any case, there are software programs already in place," the analyst said. "The NSA has been using hacking programs for emails, cell phones, computers, and surveillance systems for years. So, it's not necessarily a new concept."

"It's a new concept for someone who would now be called a civilian... albeit a very dangerous one."

"But not if he's hooked up with someone. And if this is how he's getting his info, hacking emails and such, then he's got someone with some serious skills."

"How many people outside the NSA would know how to do things like that?" Lawson said.

"There are some people who probably could. It'd take a long time to perfect a system and for it to go undetected. But there are some people, hacktivist groups, things like that who could probably create something. Or he's got someone who used to work for the NSA who's already familiar with and knows the system."

"We could be veering a little bit off course here. Let's first figure out how to apprehend Smith, then we can figure out his infrastructure afterwards."

"How about we set some type of trap for him?" the analyst asked.

"What do you have in mind?"

"If we assume we're right and he's got some type of

hacking program, then let's set up some fake accounts and emails and see if we can set something up for him."

Lawson nodded, thinking it just might work. "How long would it take you to do something like that?"

"Probably a good part of the day. If his intel is as good and as deep as we think it is, you can be sure they do a good background check on their victims before they target them. We'll have to set up emails, some false identities, background info, create criminal histories and the like. It's gonna have to be detailed and look authentic," the analyst said. "Because if he's got a computer guy, and he's as good as we think he is, he's double and triple checking this stuff. They're not gonna make a move on anything until they're absolutely sure it's legit."

"OK. Do it," Lawson said. "Make it good. Take as much time as you need to get it right. Because one thing's for sure, we might not get another crack at this. If they realize it's us and we're setting a trap, the door is closing and we're never getting it open again."

As Lawson and her team started creating false identities and documents to set their trap, Recker and Jones continued working as they usually did, completely unaware of the impending danger they were about to face. During the early morning commute, Jones took Recker back down to the area of the jewelry store so he could pick his car back up. Once they did that, they went back to the office to figure out their next steps. Though Jones headed straight there to begin working, Recker stopped for breakfast for them both. When he got back, Jones had the television on and was watching the news. Recker didn't really need to say anything since he noticed the jewelry store in the background of the reporter who was on camera.

"I take it they're discussing last night's events?" Recker asked.

"Astute observation."

"Anything interesting?"

"I guess it would depend on your definition of interesting," Jones said.

"Was my name mentioned?"

"Oh yes. The witnesses in the store positively identified you to both the police and the media."

"Well, like I told you, without the store clerk I don't know if I would've made it out of there. That reporter could've been standing outside of the police precinct talking about my capture."

"I know. I guess it's something to be thankful for. But regardless, in the beginning of the broadcast they plastered your picture on the screen the police released the other day. You know as well as I do the CIA is getting wind of this right now."

"Probably."

"So, what do you want to do?" Jones solemnly asked.

Recker shrugged. "I don't think my position has changed any."

"You know they're coming."

"Yeah," Recker sighed.

"Then why do you insist on staying here?"

"I dunno. I guess running doesn't have much appeal

to me. I've never been someone who likes to hide somewhere."

"I know that. But if we don't do something, then we both know at some point, they will find you."

"You know, when I was waiting at the jewelry store, I was thinking maybe it'd be smart if you started looking at some other candidates," Recker said.

"What?"

"Well, in case I get locked up or killed, it's gonna take a while before you can get someone else acclimated."

"Well how about if we don't let it come to that and pack up and move somewhere else?" Jones asked, pressing home his point from their previous discussions.

"David, the only one in the hot seat is me. You don't need to continually pack up and move every couple years. While I'm around, the CIA is a threat. Always will be. Do you really want to move every time there's a threat?"

"Of course not, but..."

"The more times you move, the more likely it is you're gonna make a mistake somewhere along the way."

"Well I disagree there," Jones said, trying not to boast about his skills.

"If you have to move to a new place, this isn't exactly a simple operation which can be put up and taken down at the snap of a finger," Recker said. "You have to learn the people, contacts, everything starts all over again. Mistakes will get made trying to get familiar with everything."

"Perhaps. But it's better than the alternative of just

sitting here and waiting for you to get placed in a body bag."

"There's only so many times you can move."

"The world's a big place, Michael. There are infinite possibilities."

"Even if that's so, and even if the CIA never finds me, have you given thought about bringing another person on board?"

"To work alongside of us?" Jones asked, a little surprised at the question.

"Yeah."

"Hmm. It's an interesting proposition. It may have crossed my mind a time or two over the years but I can't say I have really given it much thought. Not seriously anyway."

"Maybe it's time you gave it some thought. Seriously."

"Why? Do you feel you're overworked or over-whelmed at times?"

"No, but the more people we got out there, the more people we can help," Recker said. "There are times when more bodies would make us more effective."

"But also, more people to worry about."

"We could make it work. Take tonight for instance. It was just me against four. If I had someone who could do what I do, then I could've taken two, and he could've taken two. Then the job would've been done a lot faster and I wouldn't have had to do my Houdini act at the end to escape."

"I guess there's a good point in there."

"I try to make them every now and then."

"Yes, though I wonder if you're suggesting it because

you feel it's actually a good idea and you would like the help, or because you feel like your time is coming to an end and you don't want to leave me shorthanded."

Recker didn't bother to respond and just shrugged, heading over to a computer to work on some things. They had nothing else to work on according to Jones and he figured he'd try to find out anything else he could in regard to the CIA breathing down their necks. Jones periodically glanced over to his friend, a little concerned over his state of mind. He knew Recker wasn't one who scared easily, or someone who ran from a fight, but Jones just didn't get why he wasn't more interested in getting out of there with the conditions as they were. It didn't seem like Recker was giving up or anything, but Jones just felt like he should have been more willing to consider other alternatives besides staying there and slugging it out with the secretive government agency. Recker certainly didn't appear to be someone with a death wish. But his motivations for doing anything weren't always clear.

From Recker's standpoint, after hearing of the CIA coming, his first inclination was to pack up and leave the area, set up shop somewhere else and start over again. But the more he agonized over it, the more he realized he just wasn't interested in running for the rest of his life. Though he wasn't ready to leave the world yet, he just didn't want to pick up and move every time the CIA started getting close. While he was used to the cloak and dagger world he was engrossed in, he was getting to the point where he just wanted to stay in one place. He didn't want to be a nomad and move to a new city every year or two years. Recker didn't think it was much of a life, just trying to stay one step ahead of the organization that was hunting him. And since he was now back on their radar, if there was ever any doubt they'd forgotten about him, it was now gone.

Maybe if he hadn't killed 17 yet, he would've felt different. After all, for a long time, finding and killing him was the only thing Recker was really living for. Now he had accomplished his mission, maybe Recker wasn't really living for anything. Sure, he found satisfaction in his work and helping people avoid becoming a bad statistic, but there had to be more to life than just that. Something on a more personal level. If he wasn't being hunted, maybe Mia would've been the something he needed or craved. But while the situation was the way it was, he could never put another woman's life in danger because of him. He just wouldn't. Not again.

Recker and Jones, neither of whom had much to say, worked silently for the next several hours. While Recker continued monitoring the CIA as best he could, he knew it was a losing game. There was only so much they could do from there. He knew the chances were good that he wouldn't see them until they were right on top of him. Jones was digging into the background of a few people for a few cases which were on the horizon. While he was doing that, he continued thinking about Recker's behavior and stance on not wanting to leave. Finally, he stopped working and swiveled his chair around to face his friend and pick his brain a little more.

"So, are you going to tell me what the real reason is that you don't want to leave here?" Jones said. "I know it can't be as simple as that."

"Why can't it?" Recker said, not taking his eyes off the computer.

"I don't know. Most of the time, people have more complex reasons for doing anything. It's very rarely one thing, but a mixture of thoughts that cause it."

"Maybe."

"I know you don't have a death wish. Or do you?"

Recker snickered at the suggestion. "If I had a death wish, I would've died on the battlefield last night."

"I know. If you tell me it's the honest truth that you just don't want to pick up and leave then I'll leave the subject alone. But I just don't believe it is. And considering we're in this together, and what you do affects me, I think I have a right to know the truth."

Recker sighed and finally took his attention off the computer screen. "Truthfully, I don't even know myself what the real reason is. I guess it's probably a bunch of things."

"Such as?"

"Well, part of it is the resignation that eventually they're going to find me. I mean, why keep putting it off?"

"Self-preservation is always a good reason," Jones said.

"What exactly am I preserving?"

"Your life, your work. It's a good start."

"Living on the run isn't much of a life," Recker said.

"I've never heard you talk like this before."

"I guess it's just the realization..."

"What?"

"I don't know." Recker sighed. "I guess part of me figures... I don't even know what I'm saying."

"Does this have anything to do with Mia's recent situation?" Jones said.

"Maybe a little."

After a few seconds of thinking, Jones thought he might've stumbled upon it. "Are you feeling sorry for yourself?"

"No."

"Is it about Carrie?"

"I dunno."

"Mike, you're going to have to start explaining what it is you're actually feeling."

"Explaining my feelings isn't something I'm exactly good at or used to," Recker said.

"Yes, I'm aware. But give it a try."

"I guess it's like you said, a little bit of everything. After Carrie died, the only thing that kept me going was finding the person who was responsible for it. For three years, it was my life."

"And now that's finished, you're finding it hard to have a purpose to keep going," Jones said.

"I guess so."

"Carrie's death has been avenged, Mia's moving on, and there's nothing else on a personal level to keep you moving forward."

"Yeah."

"What about the work we're doing? The people we're helping, the people who are alive and well because of you, doesn't it mean anything to you?"

"Of course it does. But there's gotta be more to life than just going around and shooting people every week, doesn't there?"

With his weary outlook, Jones could now obviously tell what the problem was. Recker needed some deeper meaning in his own life. He'd spent most of his adult life helping and protecting others so he never thought about his own needs much. Then, when he finally did and met Carrie, it was ripped away from him. He was ready to leave the life he led behind once before, and Jones surmised he might wish to do it again, or at least have a life outside of his work. But he was stuck in the neutral zone where he didn't want to be alone anymore, but he didn't want to bring someone close to him either.

"At the risk of sounding unsympathetic to your problems, Mike, at some point you're going to have to make a decision on what it is you truly want."

"Don't you ever get tired of being cooped up in here most hours of the day, seven days a week?" Recker said.

"Maybe once in a great while. But for the most part, no, it really doesn't bother me. I made the decision a long time ago when I first decided on going ahead with this operation, this would be what the rest of my life was like. And I was OK with it. I knew going into this that love or relationships would be non-existent. They would be for other people. The people I'm trying to help. I put to rest any ideas I may have ever had about leading a normal life, having a wife, having kids, buying a house, all the other normal things normal people do. I think your biggest problem is, that you had a taste of what another life could be, you liked it, and you've never let go of it."

Recker just nodded as Jones continued, not really knowing how to respond, but basically agreeing with his sentiments.

"But the life you started to build with Carrie is gone, Mike. She's gone. You've never really accepted her death. No matter what you've done, where you've gone, who you've killed, who you've met, you've never let her go. You've got to move on and accept the life you now have or choose a different path."

"I know."

"The life you had with Carrie is never coming back. You're never getting those feelings back. And unless you're planning on sweeping Mia off her feet, which I agree would be unwise, then you need to fully immerse yourself in the life we now lead and embrace it whole-heartedly."

Recker agreed with everything Jones had said to him and felt he was right on the mark. He still held on to the feelings he had when he was with Carrie and always somehow wanted those feelings to return, just not at the price she paid for them.

"I've already taken the liberty of scouting a few other cities we could relocate to if you're of mind," Jones said.

The Professor pulled out a file folder from underneath a mountain of other papers and slid it along the desk for Recker to peruse. Recker, intrigued at what Jones had come up with, curiously lifted the folder and started looking at the options.

Recker read the names aloud as he looked at the list. "Baltimore, Boston, Atlanta, Dallas, Denver, Los Angeles, Las Vegas, San Diego, Detroit, Houston."

"I figured it would be wise to leave off New York since Centurion is located there and Chicago since it's my hometown," Jones said.

"What made these cities fit the bill?"

"Large enough to blend in, and large enough to make a difference. Though if you have other suggestions or preferences, then I'm more than willing to discuss it."

"No, these are fine."

"So, does it mean you will agree to a move?" Jones asked.

"I'll consider it."

"Soon I hope."

"I don't want to move just yet."

"When?"

"Let's finish up whatever we have in the pipeline here first," Recker said. "I know you've been looking at a few things."

"So, after we clean it all up, you'll agree to go?"

Though he still didn't really want to leave, Recker begrudgingly agreed and nodded his head. "As long as everything here is finished up. And I guess I'd need to give Mia a proper goodbye."

12

R ecker had called Mia and asked to meet her for lunch. It'd been a couple of days since he agreed to Jones' proposition of moving to a new city and he wanted to tell her in person he was going. He didn't want to tell her on the phone, or through a voice mail or a text message. He wanted to see her face and look into her eyes as he told her. He wasn't exactly sure how Mia would take the news, but he imagined she wouldn't be too sad or devastated considering she'd found someone new. That should've taken the sting out of it, if there was any. Recker and Jones were trying to get their last few cases squared away before Recker met Mia at the hospital.

"You know, it's probably for the best anyway that you're going far away from her," Jones said.

"Why?"

"Well, her new boyfriend for one."

"What about him?"

"Well, considering he's met you and seen your face,

and the face of The Silencer has been bandied about in the news recently, don't you think eventually he'd put two and two together?"

"Hmm. You know I hadn't really thought about it."

"Well, think about it. Considering he's a lawyer, even though not a criminal one, but still, at some point your picture will find its way in front of him. Even if he's just hobnobbing it up with other lawyers or watching TV or doing research. Somehow he'll find those pictures."

"Yeah, probably."

"Yes, and when he does, he'll have some very pointed questions for Mia, don't you think?" Jones said.

"She wouldn't tell him anything," Recker said.

"Maybe not at first. But if their relationship progresses a year or two from now and marriage is on the horizon, you really think she'd lie to him to protect you still?"

"Good point."

"And if he were to find out next week by chance, don't you think it'd put her relationship in peril, with him wondering how she knows you?"

Recker raised his eyebrows and nodded, putting his hands in the air, wondering why he was still being bombarded with questions on the matter.

"David, I already said you made a good point. I got it," Recker said.

"Well I'm just saying."

"I know. You're right. If the guy realizes who I am, then he also might start digging into things, might talk to the wrong person, then it would also put Mia in the crosshairs since she'd be the last known link to me."

"What do you think you'll say to her?" Jones asked.

"Damned if I know."

"Well you've been thinking about this for several days now, surely you must've come up with something by this time."

"Only thing I got so far is hi."

"Hi. That's it?"

"How do you come out and tell someone who saved your life and patched you up that you're moving in a week to someplace far, far, away and I can't tell her where it is for her own protection?" Recker said.

"OK, I'll help you out. How about this?" Jones said. "Say, Mia, the police are getting close to me and I have to move. How you like it?"

"And people think I'm the insincere one?"

"No good? How about this? Mia, the CIA is just about here to kill me so I have to go now."

"Who says you don't have a sense of humor?" Recker asked.

"I wasn't aware anyone said any such thing."

Recker just mumbled, unimpressed by any of the suggestions Jones had offered. Mia was a special person to him and he didn't want to be blunt or cold-blooded about it. He figured she'd still want to keep in touch somehow, either phone, or text, or email, all of which was OK with him, as long as it couldn't be traced back to his location. If anyone ever did figure out she was the last link to him, they could hack into her accounts to find him.

Once Recker got to the hospital and made his way to the cafeteria, he found their usual table in the back of it and waited for her to arrive. He was a little nervous about telling her his news. Outside of Jones, she was the only person who meant anything to him. When they first met, Recker only wanted her to remain a casual acquaintance, someone he could use in emergencies. But she obviously became so much more. She became a good friend, someone he could rely on and trust. Things which didn't come so easily to him. And he wasn't eager to let her go.

As Mia entered the cafeteria and saw her friend sitting there waiting, she could tell by his body language something was up. He just looked different. For one, he was looking down at the table and tapping his fingers on it. She could never remember a time when Recker did that. It was the first giveaway. As she approached the table, he never even lifted his head to look at her. His mind was obviously elsewhere. Instead of sitting down across from him, Mia walked up beside him and put her hand on his shoulder.

"You OK?" she asked, keeping her tone light and pleasant.

Recker's concentration was broken by her touch, and he looked up at her and smiled. "Yeah, I'm fine."

"OK. You look like something's on your mind."

"Yeah."

Concerned with what she was about to hear, Mia walked back around the table and sat across from him.

"What's the matter?" she asked.

"Nothing's the matter per se. Just some things I wanted to talk to you about."

"Oh. OK. When you asked about meeting me for lunch today it didn't sound like just a social thing."

Recker leaned his head forward and rubbed the side of his face as he tried to figure out how to begin. "Yeah, um, it's not I guess."

Seeing as how she'd never seen him so nervous before, Mia was starting to get really concerned. "Mike, you're starting to scare me, what is it?"

"I don't really know how to say it."

"Just say something."

"David was actually giving me some ideas, and at the time they seemed totally ridiculous, but now, now maybe they weren't so bad," Recker said.

"Why would David need to give you ideas on what to say? This is really bad, isn't it?"

"I guess he was right. There's really no other way around it but to just come out and say it."

Mia leaned forward, hardly able to take the suspense already. She put her elbows on the table and placed her hands on both sides of her temple as she braced herself for the news.

"Oh boy," she whispered.

"I guess I'll just say it. By the way, how's, uh, what's his name doing?" Recker asked.

"Josh? He's fine."

"Oh. Good. Everything good with you guys so far?"

"Yeah, great, like you care. Mike, will you please tell me what you have to say before I go crazy and slap you!"

In the end, he wound up just blurting it out. "I'm leaving."

Mia didn't respond at first and just continued to look at him with sort of a blank stare, like she didn't believe what she just heard. "What?"

"I'm leaving."

"What do you mean you're leaving? That's it? Leaving what? Where? When?"

"I'm leaving Philadelphia," he said.

Mia was stunned by the news. Her mouth fell open as she took her hands off her head and leaned back in her chair. She just looked at him for a minute, unsure what to say. Recker didn't quite know what else to say either and took turns between looking at her and glancing down at the table. Mia cleared her throat then coughed before coming up with something.

"Umm, when, uh, you say you're leaving, you mean, uh... for good?"

"Yeah, probably," Recker said.

Mia looked down at the table, not only stunned, but very disappointed in the news. "So, uh, when did you decide this?"

"I guess a few days ago. David and I have been talking about it for a while and it just seemed like now was the time."

"So why? Why now suddenly?" Mia asked.

"Well it's not really sudden. There's a lot of things which have gone into it."

"Mike, please don't shut me out now," she said, pleading with him. "If you're going away and leaving, probably for good, then please just be honest with me and tell me why. I mean, after all we've been through, and the things we've done for each other, just give me that much. Don't give me some crappy answer which just leaves me with more questions."

Recker looked away from her momentarily and

thought about her request. Though he wasn't planning on telling her the exact truth, he figured she was right and she had the right to know.

"I'm starting to get a lot of attention here," Recker said.

"From who? The police? Because of those press conferences and pictures released of you?"

"Partly."

"You've never really concerned yourself with the police much before."

"I know. It's not just them though."

"Then what?"

"The CIA knows I'm here," he said. "They're coming for me. If they're not here already."

"What?" Mia asked, her voice raising in obvious concern of his well-being. "Umm, how do you know?"

"Well, it's complicated, but the best way I can describe it is, David built a sophisticated software program that hacks into the CIA computers and lifts information from them. Last week we found something with my name on it," Recker said.

"What was it?"

"Memos between various agencies, including the one I used to work for, and the CIA Director. They're looking into things, one of which is where I am."

"What makes you think they know where you are?" Mia said.

"Mia, these are extremely smart people who know how to find things if they look hard enough. If they haven't seen the picture of me the police have, then they will soon enough. Believe me, I used to work there, I know how it plays. If they're not already in the city, they will be quickly."

"Where would you go?"

"I don't know yet. We're still talking about it."

"Wow," Mia said, wiping her eyes as the tears started forming. "It's um, I just wasn't prepared for this."

"I know. I wanted to come tell you in person. I figured it'd be better this way."

"Well, thank you."

"Plus, it'll be easier on you this way," Recker said.

"Easier on me? How?"

"Well, with your new boyfriend. With my picture getting out there, I'm sure he'll eventually come across it, especially with him being a lawyer. It's bound to happen."

"I could handle him. You wouldn't have to worry about it."

"I know. But you shouldn't have to keep secrets or anything. It's not a good recipe for starting a relationship."

"And here I thought I was having a pretty good day." Mia laughed, trying to hide her sorrows. "I feel like you just told me my pet died or something."

"I'm sorry."

"No, it's not your fault. You obviously have to do what you feel you have to do. I just wish there was another way."

"I wish there was," Recker said.

"Will this be the last time I see you?"

Recker put his hands in the air, hoping to put a positive spin on it. "You never know. Maybe I'll be back one day."

"Can I still text you and call you or are you off limits?" Mia asked.

"My phone should be untraceable so you should still be able to."

"I guess that's something."

"Hey, a few months will go by and you'll get so busy with work and Josh you'll eventually forget what I even look like," Recker said with a smile.

"I really doubt it."

The two of them continued sitting there for another ten or fifteen minutes, reminiscing about some of the times they had shared over the past few years. Neither really wanted to be the one to end their talk first, knowing what would happen right after it. But eventually, Mia had to get back to work. Even though she was now in a relationship with another man, she'd never forget the feelings she had for him and how she hoped they'd eventually wind up together. And though she tried to tell herself she no longer had those feelings for him, they were still there. She just didn't show them anymore. As Mia stood to head back to work, Recker rose from his seat as well. They each walked around the table to the side and embraced in a big hug, Mia squeezing him tight. As Recker held her in his arms, his face drifted down to the top of her hair. He loved the scent of her perfume and wished this was a moment they would have always had. But it wasn't to be and he couldn't dwell on it anymore. As they separated, Mia gave him a final kiss on the cheek.

"I'll miss you," she said.

"Me too. You make sure you take care of yourself, OK?"

"I'll try. Who am I gonna get now to rescue me from vacant buildings and stuff?"

Recker smiled. "Well, hopefully you'll never have to worry about that stuff again."

"Yeah."

Mia smiled at him and started backpedaling, not wanting to take her eyes off him. She knew once she did, and she left the cafeteria, she most likely would never see him again. Eventually, though, she knew she had no choice but to turn around and leave. As she walked through the opened cafeteria doors, she turned around one last time and gave Recker a little wave. Recker put his hand up as well and watched her disappear as she exited the cafeteria. He couldn't help but think maybe she was the last good thing he'd ever have in his life. Wherever it was he and Jones wound up, he didn't think he'd do things like he did when he got here. It was kind of fortunate that one of their first cases just happened to involve a nurse, someone he could go to if he ever found himself hurt or injured. Whatever city they ended up relocating to, Recker didn't think he'd try to have another medically capable person on standby like he had with her. If something ever happened, he'd just try to deal with it himself, or find some underground type of doctor who'd been disbarred or did things on the side for the more criminally inclined crowd. Bringing someone decent into his world now seemed like a bad idea.

Dejectedly, Recker left the hospital and drove back to the office. Before getting there, he drove around aimlessly for a little bit, hoping to clear his mind some. Though he'd only been in town for around three years, it felt like home for him. It was the longest time he'd ever spent in one spot at any time in his life. Even when he was with Carrie in Florida, he usually would only spend a few weeks at a time there before going out on a job. He felt a little sad that he had to pick up and go somewhere else. He just hoped this wouldn't be an every other year thing with having to move. After soaking in the city streets for close to an hour, Recker finally made his way back to the office. Jones was curious how his lunch and talk with Mia went.

"So, how'd it go?" Jones said.

Recker shrugged. "I dunno. As well as can be expected I guess."

"How'd she take it?"

"She didn't break down and cry if that's what you're asking. Though it looked like she wanted to."

"I'll miss her too," Jones said. "Obviously not in the same way you will, but I'll miss her just the same."

"Yeah."

"Quite likely the last friend I'll ever have," Jones said. "Well, other than you I mean."

"Yeah, me too."

"Do you think you two will keep in touch?"

"Yeah. At first anyway. After a while, I don't know. You know what they say about friends and long-distance relationships," Recker said.

"No, I don't. What do they say?"

"They slowly drift apart. I'd imagine we'd be no different. It's tough to be a part of someone's life from a few hundred or a few thousand miles away."

"Yeah, I guess so."

"Did you give any more thought to where you wanna go?" Recker asked. "Not Houston. It's too hot. Plus, I wouldn't be able to wear my signature trench coat."

"Fine. I think we should abandon the East Coast and try the Midwest or West Coast," Jones said.

"I could agree to that. How about Detroit?"

"Why Detroit?"

"I dunno. They got a pretty big crime problem there, don't they?" Recker asked. "Seems like we'd do some good there."

"Detroit? Yes, I suppose it would work for me."

"How soon do you think it'll take to set up shop again?"

"Maybe a week, two at the most."

"Why so long?"

"Well, I need to scout locations for an office space," Jones said. "Plus, I have to change the server locations I get my information from. It takes time to do the things I do, Michael. I don't just snap my fingers and voila, magic appears. It actually takes some work and skill to do the things I do."

"I know, I know, I was just asking."

"I didn't just set up this operation in a couple days you know. It took thorough and meticulous planning."

"I bet. Speaking of new things, did you give any more thought to my suggestion of bringing on another guy?" Recker said.

"Guy? Why not a girl?"

"Just a figure of speech. Guy, girl, it, I don't care. As long as whoever's brought in can talk, shoot, and fight, and isn't a douchebag, I don't care who it is. As long as they're capable."

"I know, I was just kidding. But anyway, yes, I have given it some thought."

"And?"

"I'm not opposed to the idea. I would just like to get established somewhere else for a while before actually considering applications," Jones said. "Maybe a few months or so anyway."

"I'm surprised."

"Why is that?"

"I really didn't think you were too interested in the idea of bringing someone else on board," Recker said.

"Well, some of the points you made had some merit to them. It would make some assignments easier, as it were, but just because we might be interested in bringing someone else in, doesn't mean someone's just going to fall in our lap, just like that. It might take months or even years to find someone. I don't want to add just any old person into the fold. They have to have the right qualifications and background."

"You mean someone as loving, cheerful, and jovial as me?" Recker said with a grin.

"I don't think the world is ready for a carbon copy of you."

"That almost hurts my feelings."

"I'm sure."

"Hey, while we're on the subject of new things, how about a pet?"

"A pet?"

"Yeah, you know, something to hang around the office

all day with. Something to take our mind off things every once in a while and unwind, de-stress."

"You've got to be joking."

"No, why?"

"I can barely handle you and you want to bring in an animal I have to take care of?" Jones asked.

"You don't have to by yourself. We'll all pitch in."

"What has gotten into you? First you wanna bring in another person, then you want to bring in a pet, what's next, a baby?"

"Sorry David, you're not really my type."

"Well thank goodness for that."

"So, the pet is out?"

"I really don't think we have enough time for it, do you?"

"Well, depends on what it is. Dogs are probably out. I like them, but they need more attention than other animals," Recker said. "We'd probably need something like cats, or fish, or maybe hamsters or something."

"No, no hamsters. I don't think I could work properly hearing them running around on a little wheel or whatever it is."

"Cats?"

"No, with our luck we'd wind up with one of those cats who likes to lay on your lap as you're working or lay on one of my computers or something."

"Fish?"

"I don't know, I guess I'll think about it."

"Oh, we finally found an animal you like."

"I don't dislike animals, Michael," Jones said. "I'm just not sure we can give one the attention it deserves."

"You should watch yourself, David. You're starting to sound like a grouchy old man," Recker said, grinning again.

Though Jones obviously knew Recker was kidding with the animal suggestions, or at least he hoped he was, he wasn't really enjoying this side of his friend. He preferred the violent, brooding partner he'd grown accustomed to.

"Don't you have somewhere else to go or anything?" Jones asked.

"No, not really. Why? Are you trying to get rid of me?"

"To be honest... yes."

Recker laughed, appreciating his honesty. "Well, can't get mad at you for the truth."

"Don't you have someone you could shoot or something?"

"Seriously?"

"No, not seriously."

"Oh, because I could probably go out and find someone if you really want me to," Recker said.

"I honestly have no doubts of that. But I'd really prefer if you stay out of the spotlight if possible."

"You know how I struggle with that."

"Well, hopefully it's something in which you'll improve at our next destination."

"Yeah, well, I wouldn't count on it too much if I were you."

"Believe me, I'm not."

"Ye of little faith."

"Faith can move mountains, Michael. But it can't cure someone who's gun-happy."

13

For the next several days, Jones spent a considerable amount of time trying to wrap things up in Philadelphia, while also scouting out possible locations in Detroit they could use as a base of operations. Something like what they had now was ideal, but he was open to other possibilities as well. Looking at potential offices over the internet was a bit problematic but just about possible. Thanks to the power of the internet as well as pictures of residential or commercial spaces for sale, Jones could get a decent enough handle on what was available. With the increased scrutiny, albeit more on Recker, he didn't want to take the chance of traveling back and forth to a new city and putting their plans at risk, no matter how small or remote the odds were. While he was taking care of the logistics of their planned move, Recker continued taking on a few small cases. Nothing was especially major or time absorbing, just minor things he could take care of relatively quickly.

"Did you start cleaning out your apartment yet?" Jones said.

"Have you ever seen my apartment?"

"Well you know I have. I've been in there many times."

"But have you actually looked at it?" Recker asked.

"I don't get your meaning."

"Well, if you've actually looked at my apartment, then you'd know that with the amount of stuff I have it could be cleaned out and moved in about an hour."

"An hour might be pushing it slightly," Jones said.

"Anything I need could be put in my SUV and I'd still have plenty of room to spare."

As they were discussing their moving plans, an alert came in on Jones' computer. He slid his chair over to the computer and started checking out the information as it came on screen. By his mannerisms, mumbling, and facial expressions, Recker could tell it was something big. At least bigger than the minor issues they'd been dealing with over the past week.

"What is it?" Recker asked.

"It appears we've got a hit on a potential bank robbery."

"When?"

"Looks like tomorrow around noon," Jones said.

"Nice. Haven't interrupted a good bank robbery in a long time. What kind of players are we dealing with?"

"Pulling them up now," Jones said, looking over the information before talking about it. "Looks like another four-man crew."

"Wonderful. Can't get enough of those," Recker said.

Jones was staring hard at that screen, deciphering the information. "That's not good."

"What's the matter?"

"One of the text messages I intercepted indicates they're quite willing to kill people inside. Perhaps a police matter?"

"No, I'll take care of it," Recker said.

"Are you sure? This crew looks like they're even more violent and dangerous than the last one."

"One last going away party I guess."

Jones pulled up the picture of the bank that was supposed to be hit and they started going over the background of the team behind the crime in waiting. Each member of the squad had lengthy and violent criminal histories. They were like the crew Recker took out at the jewelry store not too long ago. But the longer they looked over the impending robbery, something kept tugging at Recker that just didn't seem right.

"This doesn't feel right," Recker said.

"Why? What's the matter?"

"I dunno. It's just... it just doesn't seem like the best bank you could hit."

"Well, I'm sure they have their reasons for it," Jones said.

"I'm sure they do. It's not a large bank, it's at the end of a shopping center, it's not near a major highway," Recker said.

Jones stopped him before he could keep going. "Mike, you're thinking logically and like someone who doesn't rob banks. These people are not necessarily logical. If they were, they wouldn't do what their history says they have."

"I know. I just always try to place myself in their shoes to figure out how I would do it."

"Yes, but you also know that sometimes it's just not possible to figure out how other people's minds work."

"Yeah. Hopefully, this is the last big job we take on before we go."

"I have a feeling it will be," Jones said.

Recker and Jones spent the rest of the day multitasking. Recker began formulating a plan as to how to stop the bank robbery, while Jones continued with the impending move of their business. As Recker studied, he still found it strange how the crew was targeting that specific bank. It was a local community bank carrying a fraction of the money a few larger banks would have, several of which were only a few minutes away. But Jones was right, any bank was a target and the crew must have had their reasons for the job.

The following morning, Recker rose early, ready to tackle the day's events. For the first time he could remember, he beat Jones into the office. Jones took it as a bad omen.

"I think something is going to go horribly wrong today," Jones said.

"Why?"

"For three years I've been the first one into the office and everything has gone fine until now. Now, on one of our last days here, with possibly the most dangerous crew we've come into contact with, you break the string and mess things up by getting here first. You're putting bad voodoo on us or something."

"Really, David? Bad voodoo?" Recker asked.

"You know what I meant."

"And everything has gone fine. You really need me to go over all the times something's gone wrong? How about the time I was shot and disappeared for a few days?"

"Well, I wouldn't classify it as going wrong," Jones said. "You're still here, aren't you? Just a minor hiccup or bump in the road. But this, you're getting us off on the wrong foot today."

"I kind of doubt I'll get killed today just because I beat you into the office."

"Let's hope not."

After quelling Jones' fears and taking care of a few last-minute details, Recker grabbed some of his favorite weapons out of the gun cabinet and left the office about 10:30am. It was a half hour drive to the bank, getting him there about an hour before the job was supposed to go down, giving him ample time to wait for his targets, as he liked to do. He was in constant communication with Jones throughout the morning through the com device in his ear.

"How's everything looking so far?" Jones asked.

"Quiet. I'm just hoping nobody sees me sitting here for an hour and thinks I'm the one robbing the bank."

"That would qualify as a disaster, wouldn't it?"

Fueled by the jewelry store job, where Recker couldn't quite make up his mind on how to attack, he had already decided on a plan this time. Though he didn't think his lack of a decision at the jewelry store played any part in how things unraveled towards the end, he certainly didn't think it helped. He wasn't going to make the same mistake again here. He figured out the best strategy, and he was sticking to it. He was going to hit them as soon as he saw them arrive, hopefully killing them before they even stepped foot in the bank. The hour passed by quickly, probably because of the constant communication with Jones which kept Recker's mind off other things. As Recker looked at the time, he watched the last couple of minutes tick by until twelve o'clock hit. He did one last check of his weapons to make sure they were fully loaded, including his two handguns and his assault rifle.

Recker's eyes were diverted to the right entrance when a black cargo van pulled in and pulled up right in front of the bank's entrance.

"A van just pulled up to the bank. Think this might be it," Recker said.

"Please be careful," Jones said.

Recker jarred open his door, waiting for the bank crew to unload out of the van before he fully got out of the car, not wanting to show his hand too quickly and scare them off. Two members of the crew got out of the passenger side of the van, and with a black bag in hand, started walking toward the entrance of the bank.

"Showtime," Recker said.

He quickly got out of his car and jogged closer to the bank. Not wanting them to drive off after seeing him, Recker's first action was to shoot the tires of the van with his assault rifle to make a getaway not possible. As he scurried to the van, the driver threw a gun out the window and stuck both his hands out to indicate he was giving up. Recker thought it was a bit strange the man was giving up so quickly and without even putting up a bit of a fight. Unusual for someone with the violent background these men possessed. Recker quickly turned his attention to the men near the door, only to find they'd done the same. Their guns were on the ground, and their hands were already in the air. Recker was slightly unnerved by what was happening and took a couple of steps backwards.

"Something's not right," Recker said.

"What's wrong? What's happening?" Jones asked.

"Nothing. That's the problem. They just threw their guns down and put their hands up without even firing a shot."

"Mike, get out of there, it could be a trap."

"Yeah, I think you're right."

Just as Recker turned around and started running back to his car, sirens blared, marked and unmarked police cars raced into the shopping center from every direction. As he looked around to figure out his exit strategy among the increasing crowd, another door opened from the black van. One of the CIA assets assigned to Lawson's team took aim at Recker's chest and fired, hitting him near the shoulder. Recker grabbed at his shoulder and looked down, seeing the tranquilizer dart sticking out of it, and realized what was happening. His old friends had finally caught up with him. Breathing heavily and starting to lose consciousness, he sought to give Jones some final clarification as to what was happening so he'd know.

"David, looks like this is it," Recker said.

"Mike? Mike, what's happening?"

Recker didn't have time to respond. As soon as Jones finished, another dart made its way into Recker's chest. He dropped to a knee, feeling his last few streams of consciousness leave his body. His eyes were getting heavy and he could barely keep them open any longer. He took one last look at the black van, seeing a rifle pointed straight at him. A few seconds later, Recker finally blacked out and collapsed onto the pavement underneath him.

"Shelly, we've got him." One of the CIA officials radioed the news.

"Great, bring him to me," Lawson said.

The joint CIA/police raid was now officially over. With the police's help in securing the exits, Lawson kept her word that they'd take Recker off their hands. The men in the van took Recker's body and dragged it into the van and were gone within seconds. Jones, meanwhile, was frantically trying to figure out what had happened. While he couldn't be sure of anything yet, he could only assume Recker was trapped by either the police or the CIA. He immediately retraced everything they knew of the bank crew that turned out to be false. Unfathomably to him, someone pulled the wool over his eyes, and it quite possibly had cost Recker his freedom or his life.

As Jones panicked and started doing some computer work to figure out what happened, Recker was being taken to a facility the CIA had rented for the week. As soon as Lawson figured out how they would trap Recker, she knew they needed a secure place they could take him for the time being. Seeing as though they didn't have any nearby facilities they already owned, she found a semi-remote location in a former shipping business inside a business industrial park. It'd work perfectly since they'd only need it for a day or so.

About five hours after being taken there, Recker finally opened his eyes, only to find he was sitting with his hands behind his back and handcuffed to a chair. There was no doubt he was now in the hands of the CIA. This was their MO. Sitting by himself, tied up in an empty, dimly lit room, this was their style. After a few minutes, a door opened, and a woman started walking toward him. She sat in the empty chair a few inches across from him. It wasn't quite what Recker had expected. He figured when he was caught, assuming he wasn't shot and killed first, his final interrogation would be handled by someone he knew from Centurion.

"Hi, John. Is that what you're still going by these days or is it something else now?"

"Whatever you wanna call me is fine." Recker smiled, not seeming a bit nervous about his situation. "I can be whoever you want me to be."

"My name is Shelly."

"Nice to meet you."

Lawson returned his smile, impressed with her prisoner's calm and pleasant demeanor, who didn't seem the slightest bit anxious. "You seem awfully calm for someone in your situation."

"Well, not much else I can do right now, is there? I mean, you didn't tie my feet together, so it is theoretically possible that I could strangle you with them, but I'll wait a little while to see what you have to say first."

"Confident."

"I've done it before."

"After reading your file and your background info, it really wouldn't surprise me if you had," Lawson said.

"Considering Davenport isn't here, I assume he was bypassed, and they brought you in to find me?" Recker asked.

"Perceptive. So who were you talking to in the earpiece?" Lawson said.

"What earpiece?"

"The earpiece we found inside your ear when we grabbed you."

"Oh, that. Yeah, I had it linked to my iPod so I can listen to some tunes while I work," Recker said, smiling. "I find music helps calms my nerves in situations like that."

"Always play it cool and calm, huh?"

"I try."

Lawson pulled Recker's phone out of her pocket and started looking through it. Luckily, Recker had gotten in the habit of deleting all his text messages and any voice mails every day, so there wasn't anything in there for her to see. Except his contact list.

"You wanna tell me who these people are?" she asked.

"No idea," Recker said.

"Who's David?"

"Uh, pizza guy. Yeah, I don't like meeting strange people so I request the same driver all the time."

"You know we can check this out, right?"

"Wouldn't get you anywhere."

"How bout Tyrell?"

"My supplier."

"Vincent? Malloy?"

"My vet and my pharmacist," Recker said.

Lawson chuckled, getting a kick out of his responses. "How about Mia? Girlfriend?"

"Just a prostitute. Gotta get your fix on somehow, you know?"

"I'm sure."

Lawson put his phone back in her pocket then pulled out a piece of paper, which was folded up. Recker wondered what she was going to try to throw on him next. She unfolded the paper and looked at it for a few seconds before talking to him again.

"So, kind of strange you have someone like Vincent in your contact list, isn't it?" Lawson asked.

"What's strange about it?"

"Someone like you doing business with a mob boss like him? I don't see the connection."

Recker smiled. "You're not supposed to."

"Tyrell Gibson. Looks like a low-level hoodlum. What's your connection to him?"

"He gets me my toys."

"Mia Hendricks," Lawson said. "You know what's strange about her?"

"You tell me."

"She's different from the others in your list."

"Oh? How's that?"

"The others have criminal backgrounds. She doesn't."

"Maybe she's better at not being caught than them," Recker said.

"Or maybe because she's a nurse. Maybe you settled down. Maybe she means more to you than the others."

"That's a lot of maybe's."

"OK, let's talk about this David fellow," Lawson said. "We can't find a last name for him, nothing comes up through his phone number, as far as we can tell, he doesn't even exist."

"Hmm... that's strange."

"Isn't it?"

"You know, this is all very enlightening, but what is it you hope to accomplish with this?" Recker said. "You know I'm not gonna tell you anything. What exactly are you fishing for?"

"I'm curious about your life for the last few years. How exactly did you come up with this system of yours? Obviously, you have some type of program pulling information from emails or texts or phones that you can act upon."

"It's really not so complicated. I'm just fighting crime wherever I find it."

"OK. Let's move on to another topic."

"Can't wait."

"Gerry Edwards. Know him?" Lawson asked.

"Is, uh, is he on television?"

"No, he's an agent of ours who was killed in an airport in Ohio."

"That's a shame," Recker said. "Dangerous profession, isn't it?"

"You wouldn't happen to know anything about it, would you?"

"Afraid not."

"And you didn't know he was the one who killed your girlfriend down in Florida a few years ago, right?"

"Oh, man, I've been looking for him too. Guess someone beat me to it."

Lawson couldn't help but smile, amused by Recker's sense of humor. She didn't figure getting any information out of him was going to be easy, but she was hoping he'd give her something, even if it was only one small thing she could run with. But Recker was an old hand at this, and he wasn't going to give them the satisfaction of learning a single thing about him since the day he left them. He knew what the plan was for him. They were going to try to learn as much about his friends as they could and possibly go after them, then wind up killing everybody they considered to be any kind of threat. He figured they'd leave Mia alone since they already had him, but Jones was another story. With his computer skills, and the fact he was already wanted by the NSA, he would likely be terminated along with Recker. The CIA wouldn't take the chance of leaving Jones alone then hoping he didn't come back for some type of revenge. Recker, though, wasn't going to give them anything on Jones, no matter what kind of technique they used on him. He knew them all and was ready for whatever they threw at him. But he was hoping to bypass all the nonsense and just go straight to the part where they killed him. He didn't want a long goodbye.

"Excuse me, you seem like a very nice person, but can we just get on with the killing," Recker said.

"What killing?"

"Mine. I hate dragging things out."

"What makes you think that's what's going to happen?" Lawson asked.

"Listen, I know the game, I know how it works. You wanna pump me for whatever information I can give and when I run dry, you finish the game. I'm not gonna play."

"Well, regardless of what you think you know, you don't. Let me explain to you exactly what's going on here. We know Gerry Edwards killed your girlfriend, Carrie. We also believe that several months afterwards you relocated to Philadelphia. How, we don't know. It is my personal belief that you hooked up with some computer geek who gets you information on what criminals or jobs to go on. I also think he found out where Edwards lived and passed the information on to you. You've been looking for him all this time then you went down there and killed him."

"Nice theory," Recker said.

"John, I know you don't trust me, and that's fine, I understand. I wouldn't trust me either in your shoes. I've looked over your package, your background, every mission you've been on, the doctors you've talked to, everyone who's ever had a connection to you since you've been in the CIA."

"And what'd you find?"

"I found someone who was wrongly terminated, attempted anyway," Lawson said. "But what you think is happening here, isn't what's happening."

Recker wasn't sure what the woman was talking about, but he was skeptical about anything she said. He figured this was the nice guy routine to get him to open up. She was good, because it almost worked. But Recker wasn't falling for it. By his facial expression, Lawson could see he was less than impressed by anything she was saying. If she wanted him to even remotely trust her, she was going to have to make an extreme move. One that could cost her life if she was wrong about him. She got up and walked around behind Recker, just standing there for a minute. Recker was starting to feel a little uneasy, thinking this might be it. He was waiting to hear the click of a gun, or feel the sharp steel of a knife. Instead, he felt his hands become free as the rope bonding them together was untied. He brought his arms around in front of him and he rubbed his wrists as Lawson walked back around where he could see her.

"I don't want to kill you," Lawson said. "If I did, you'd be dead already."

"What makes you think you're safe enough that I won't do it to you?"

"Because I'm trusting you won't. I'm not Sam Davenport. I'm hoping that has something to do with it. And if none of that does, then there are several men outside the door who would kill you if they hear something doesn't sound right. And if none of those do it for you, then maybe your curiosity will, wondering what it is I want."

"I'm listening," Recker said, confirming that he was indeed curious.

Untying his hands was a move Recker wasn't expecting. There he was sitting in a chair without a single restraint to hold him back. Yet here was this woman talking to him like they'd known each for a long time, someone who knew what he was capable of, but didn't appear to be afraid of him in the least. It was a strange play on her part from his perspective.

"I was brought in to find you because Centurion believed you were responsible for Gerry Edwards' death," Lawson said. "After a few months of no progress, I was brought in from another agency to find you, or his killer, or both if it turned out it was you."

"Well congratulations."

"But I don't think you're a bad guy, or you're a threat, or you should've been rubbed out in London."

Recker just looked at her, wondering where she was going with this.

"I was tasked with bringing you in, one way or another. But like I said, I don't believe you're a bad guy. I don't want to bring you in dead."

"Honestly, you seem like a nice woman, but I don't wanna go back alive. Someone in Centurion will find a way to kill me anyway, or they'll stash me in some dark hole for thirty years. Neither one is an appealing proposition to me," Recker said.

"I asked Director Roberts personally if I could bring you back into the fold, if he would sign off on it, and he indicated he would," Lawson said.

Recker was a little astonished. Coming back in to work for them was literally the last thing he would have ever thought of, if he ever thought of it at all. It was so far-fetched to him he had never even considered it a possibility. Recker tilted his head back and looked away from her, thinking about what she just said. Lawson could tell he was taken aback.

"I understand you would still have trust issues," Lawson said. "We can put you in another division, another project, we can work with you to get you acclimated again."

"Why? Why go through all this trouble for me?"

"Like I said, I read your file. I didn't think what happened to you was right. And I believe you're someone who still has a lot to offer. There's a lot of things you could've done to hurt us, Centurion, the United States, but you didn't do any of them. It says a lot about you."

"I understand the way things work," Recker said, beginning to open up. "There was only one person I really had an issue with."

"Gerry Edwards?"

"Yeah. You're right. I killed him."

"How'd you find him?" Lawson said.

"That's as much as I'll reveal. What now?"

"Now I close off his file. The rest depends on you."

"And if I say no?" Recker asked.

"I'm really hoping you'll see things my way."

"I dunno. Trusting anyone within this agency is a lot to ask."

"I know. It'll be a process. But it's one I think is doable."

"What makes you think I won't say yes then when I'm in some foreign country, I won't just go off the reservation again?"

"I've thought of that," Lawson said. "There are ways around it."

Recker chuckled. "Any tracking devices you plant inside me I'll find a way to get out."

"Somehow that wouldn't surprise me."

Recker took another minute to just think about the offer just presented to him. He couldn't pretend there wasn't a piece of it that was appealing to him. Lawson struck him as being credible and believable. He was sure she was trustworthy to most other people, but for him, it wouldn't come in the matter of a few minutes. Lawson leaned forward and put her hand on one of Recker's knees. She could see he was conflicted and tried to set his mind at ease a little.

"John, you wouldn't have to run anymore," she said. "It'd be over for you."

"I don't know if I can do it anymore. That part of my life is over."

"You prefer running around in the shadows of the night, shooting low lifes, and avoiding cops?"

"It's not just that."

"Mia? This David person?"

Recker sighed, unsure he could explain it in a way that would make sense and she would understand. "It's more than that. I feel like I've made a home here. There's people here I care about. Even when I was with the agency, towards the end, I really didn't want to be there anymore."

As Recker continued to think about the offer, the less appealing it became. His heart just wasn't in doing that kind of work anymore. He knew what declining the offer meant, but he had to be true to himself and be honest with Lawson.

"Listen, I appreciate you going to the trouble of finding me and not killing me on sight, but I just can't do it," Recker said. "I think that ship has sailed. There's no going back for me now. You seem like you've been upfront with me and I'll return the courtesy. If it means you have to put me out of my misery, then you have to do what you have to do."

"So, I guess there's no way to talk you into it?"

"No. I couldn't even pretend to say I prefer my old life to now."

Lawson was disappointed in his answer as she really thought she could've convinced him to come back to the agency. She wasn't ready to give up on him though. Seeing how he hesitated a few times, and he genuinely seemed to think about it, she took it as a sign that he wasn't a completely lost cause. Working with some of the agents she had with Project Specter, she was used to dealing with rejection at first from stubborn and bull-headed agents. They continued their dialogue for several more minutes, though Lawson wasn't getting very far. Suddenly, gunfire erupted from just beyond the other side of the door. Recker and Lawson both turned their heads toward the door, startled by the development.

"Is that your team coming for you?" Lawson asked, getting her gun out.

"My team isn't violent," Recker said. "How many men you got out there?"

"Three."

The two of them stood and looked around the room to see if there was something they could get behind to protect themselves, but there wasn't. Whatever, and whoever was coming, they'd have to deal with them head on.

"You have another gun?" Recker asked.

"No."

"I hope you can use that."

"I'm adequate," Lawson said, not very confident in her abilities.

Recker looked at her, thinking they were in serious trouble. "Great."

After a few more minutes of sporadic gunfire, the guns eventually stopped. Recker and Lawson stood there waiting, hearts thumping, sweat running down the sides of their heads, wondering what was coming.

"You don't happen to want me to hang on to the gun, do you?" Recker asked.

"Not if it's friends of yours."

"Believe me, they're no friends of mine. Maybe I can hide next to the door, then when it swings open, I can jump them when they come in."

"Worth a try I guess," Lawson said.

Recker started walking toward the door when he stopped in his tracks as it suddenly burst open after being forcefully kicked in. An angry-looking man stood in the doorway with his gun pointed at the both of them alternately. Recker didn't recognize him, but he knew his type. He was a younger man, late twenties, bald head with a coarse beard, on the shorter side, wearing a brown suit. He came in so suddenly that it surprised Lawson and she couldn't raise her gun in time.

"Who are you?" Lawson asked.

"Maintenance man. Drop the gun."

Lawson did as the man directed and let the gun slip from her fingers, dropping onto the concrete floor. Recker knew what was about to happen. With his hands out to his side, he took a few steps back toward Lawson, thinking they only had one chance at surviving this.

"Which one of us are you here for?" Lawson asked.

The man just smiled. "Both."

"Who sent you?"

"Enough talk. It only prolongs the inevitable."

The man pointed at Recker, who dove back onto the ground for the gun. Their attacker quickly fired a shot at him. Lawson moved away from the action and toward the wall to get out of the line of fire. As Recker put his hands on the gun, he winced in pain as a bullet entered into his left shoulder. Recker shrugged off the pain long enough to spin around and fire a couple shots of his own. He also hit the man in his left shoulder, temporarily dropping the man to one knee. Recker continued firing, hitting his victim three more times, twice in the chest and once in the head as the man slumped to the ground, winding up flat on his back. Recker jumped to his feet and walked over to his victim to see if he was dead. Much to his satisfaction, he was. Lawson started walking over to him as Recker searched through the dead man's pockets. He pulled out some identification cards and looked at them briefly before handing them over to Lawson.

"Look familiar?" Recker asked.

"He's a Centurion agent," Lawson said. "What's he doing here?"

"Who knew you were coming?"

"The only person I told was..."

"Sam Davenport?"

Lawson looked at him incredulously, not believing Davenport would've actually tried to take them both out.

"Welcome to my world," Recker said to her. "Now you've joined the club."

"Are you OK?" Lawson asked, noticing the blood on his shirt and touching his shoulder.

"Yeah, I'll be fine."

"I'll take you somewhere to get it looked at."

"No, it's OK. Don't worry about it. I got someone."

"I'm sure you do. Oh, that's right, the nurse."

They stood there silently for a few moments, somewhat awkwardly as they figured out their next steps. Lawson was no longer in control of the situation, especially since her cohorts were now dead, and she no longer had possession of her gun. Recker realized he was now in power and the woman's fate lay in his hands. Lawson glanced down at the gun in his hands and wondered what he was going to do with her.

"So, what now?" Lawson asked.

Recker lifted his right arm and pointed the gun straight at her. After a brief second, he spun the gun around in his hand, holding the barrel of it. He then straightened out his arm and offered Lawson's gun back to her. She took it, and after pointing it at him for a split second, put it back in her holster.

"Looks like I've got a mess to clean up," Lawson said.

"How you gonna handle it?" Recker said.

"Well, I'd say Director Roberts is going to be very unhappy with a certain person who's in charge of a particular black ops program. Maybe he'll be the one who ends up in a deep dark hole somewhere."

"I wouldn't be opposed to that."

"I think it's safe to say nobody will be hearing from him for a very long time."

"And John Smith?" Recker asked.

Lawson thought for a minute before answering. She wasn't ready to give up on the thought of him eventually rejoining the agency. "As far as I can tell, Sam Davenport arranged the death of Gerry Edwards, just as he orchestrated the elimination of John Smith. He's innocent of all allegations against him and from what we've uncovered, he's not a threat at this time."

Recker gave her a wry smile. "Thank you."

"And maybe one day he'll come back into the fold. I'll continue to keep an eye on him."

"Well, you did find him once. Maybe you can do it again sometime."

Recker and Lawson shook hands, and she handed him back his phone. "You might need it," she said.

Recker then left the room and started making his way toward Mia's place so she could tend to his shoulder. One more time for old time's sake. Once he left, Lawson called Director Roberts and informed him of what happened so Sam Davenport could be taken into custody immediately. As Recker walked along the roadside, he called Jones to let him know he was OK and that he'd need a ride. When Jones finally pulled up alongside him, he had plenty of questions about his ordeal.

"Thank God, I never thought I'd see you again," Jones said.

"Had a few doubts myself."

"What happened?"

"Let's get to Mia's first and I'll tell you all about it," Recker said.

Jones called Mia to make sure she was at home, which thankfully she was after just finishing up her shift. He let her know he was bringing her a patient, which she could only guess was Recker. Once they got to her apartment, she was already waiting for them. She'd been periodically looking out the window, concerned about Recker's condition. When she noticed them pull up to the building, she saw Recker walking in, seeming normal, which relieved her worries a little. When they got to her door, they didn't even need to knock, as she swung it open for them as they got there. She immediately saw the blood on his shirt and just shook her head, at which Recker grinned.

"Will you never learn?" she asked innocently.

"Figured I'd leave you something to remember me by."

"This is a present I could've done without."

"Some things never change."

ABOUT THE AUTHOR

Mike Ryan lives in Pennsylvania, with his wife, and four kids. He is the bestselling author of The Silencer Series, The Cain Series, The Eliminator Series, as well as numerous other books. Visit his website at www.mikeryanbooks.com to find out more about his books, and sign up for his newsletter.

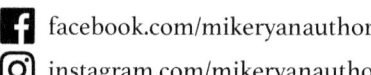 facebook.com/mikeryanauthor

instagram.com/mikeryanauthor

ALSO BY MIKE RYAN

The Eliminator Series

The Cain Series

The Ghost Series

The Extractor Series

The Brandon Hall Series

A Dangerous Man

The Crew

The Last Job

Printed in Great Britain
by Amazon